Kodak Kill Shot

A Hollywood Murder, Book 4

Cynthia Hickey

DEDICATION

To all those who love a whodunnit and characters who make you sometimes shake your head in amusement. Here's to a fun mystery!

Chapter One

"I can't work if you're in my kitchen!" Sarah Doyles, recently homeless and now resident chef of Canyon Estates, whirled to face Ruthie, my grandmother and owner of said mansion, who'd given it the family name.

"It's my kitchen." Ruthie put her hands on her slim hips and glared. "You're nothing more than the hired help, and you're getting a bit too big for your apron."

I, Kelly Canyon, unwilling guest of the upcoming party tonight, sat at the table with a cup of coffee and prepared to watch the most entertaining thing I'd seen in a month. I smiled over the rim of my cup. These two had become best friends ever since Sarah saved my life. Sarah had been there when I had to pretend to be homeless to hide from an unscrupulous cop. But even the best of friends fight like tigers once in a while, and stress was running high today.

"You're the one with the big head." Sarah wiggled her fingers. "Give me the guest list and leave me alone."

Ruthie thrust over three pages of handwritten names in Sarah's direction. "I want fancy foods. We've a guest list of one hundred and fifty." She grinned, looking rather proud of herself. "Since Kelly's and my television show, *The Hart of Crime*, is nominated for an Emmy, everyone wants to be part of our clique."

Sarah rolled her eyes. "I'll dump the first platter of fancy food over your head if you don't hire me some help."

A laugh escaped me, turning both their glares on me. I pretended to cough.

"Bad acting, girl." Ruthie shook her head and stormed from the kitchen.

"How have you lived with her for so many years?" Sarah scanned the list of names in her hand.

"She isn't so bad—"

Sarah's face darkened. "She invited Robert? That cad—the man who ruined my life? I wouldn't serve him a platter of anything but slop fit for a pig." She tossed the list on the counter.

Ruthie wouldn't dare. I retrieved the papers. Yep. She'd invited the unscrupulous businessman, Robert Doyles, Sarah's ex-husband. Oh, grandma, what were you thinking?

After setting the papers on the counter, I went to look for some explanation. Ruthie sat on a sofa, knitting needles, her new fad, clicking at a remarkable pace. I doubted whether anything useable would result from her efforts, though. All I saw emerging was a tangled mess.

"What?" She didn't look up.

"Why did you invite Robert Doyles? You know how Sarah feels about him."

Her hands stilled. "Because he provided some of the backing for our show. It's only right. She'll be in the kitchen and won't have to lay eyes on him."

"You still should have warned her."

The doorbell rang. As I headed to answer it, Ruthie said, "That would be the hired help I already got for that ungrateful woman in the kitchen."

I rolled my eyes and let in two kitchen helpers, who were informed by Ruthie that the wait staff would arrive one hour prior to the party's starting time, as would the bartender. "Are you having an open bar?" My eyes widened.

"Of course. This is Hollywood." She glanced up at me as if I'd lost my mind. "Our guests won't expect us to spare any expense. Don't worry. I'm footing the bill."

"I'll pay my share and be the official photographer, or did you hire one?"

"Of course, I hired one. You can't take photos in an evening gown. This is a formal party." Again, I got the look.

"You're always taking away my fun." Originally, my dream job was investigative journalist, and I'd worked for a tabloid until getting fired when I became a murder suspect. Then I found myself roped into acting, something I seemed to be good at, and took pictures of celebrity's pets as a side job. Now that I'd resigned myself to acting, I took photos as a hobby while trying to find my father's murderer. A full plate, but I'd never been happier. Especially since the first murder I'd gotten involved in had hooked Brock aka Handsome Hanson, Hollywood's Golden Boy, as my boyfriend.

"You can act like a star for one night, Kelly." She set down her needles. "Look at it this way. No one is likely to kill one of us at our own party."

I hoped she hadn't just jinxed us.

At eight o'clock, I stood in an ice-blue, spaghetti-strapped gown that kissed the toes of my silver sandals and greeted guests as they entered our backyard. Lights floated in the pool along with giant magnolia blossoms. Glittering white lights hung from every surface holding a strand. The place had been transformed into a fairy land.

From the rapturous looks on the guests' faces, Ruthie had outdone herself. Hollywood would be talking about the party for weeks.

Paparazzi popped cameras over the fence in hopes of scoring a shot that would land on the first page of whatever tabloid they worked for. I smiled, remembering the frenzy of those days when selling a photo of a movie star paid my rent.

A soft whistle sounded behind me and I whirled around. Brock, resplendent in a black tux, strolled my way. "You look gorgeous." His arm snaked around my waist, and he pulled me in for a kiss.

"You aren't so bad yourself." I caressed his cheek.

"Sorry I'm late, but Morgan was worried about what to wear." He grinned.

I laughed, imagining the big man being nervous about seeing Ruthie. The two were almost inseparable since the time they reconnected and she hired him as her bodyguard.

"If Ruthie does something this big over a nomination, I can't imagine what she'll throw if your show wins an Emmy."

"We'll find out soon enough." I seized his hand and led him to a pair of padded chaises in a secluded area of the yard. I shooed Shutterbug, my German shepherd, and Brutus, Brock's mastiff, from the furniture so we could sit. A yelp sounded from behind a pillow as I leaned back. I lurched up and glanced down at Sassy, Ruthie's Yorkie. "Sorry, girl."

The three dogs plopped on the ground, baleful eyes staring at us. "The chairs are for guests," I said. Sassy yelped her displeasure, bringing Ruthie running.

"What did you do to my baby?" She scooped up the dog.

"Moved her off the furniture."

"Come on, baby. Let's go find Morgan. He'll protect you from the evil Kelly." She glared at me and stormed away.

I sighed. "She's been like this all day. I think hosting this big of a party is too much for her."

"Maybe there's more on her mind than the party."

"Hmm." I accepted a glass of champagne from a waiter and leaned back. I'd received our guests, now they could fend for themselves. Schmoozing was the part of Hollywood I disliked the most, and I was no good at it.

"Come on." Brock held out his hand. "Let's walk. Let people see how beautiful you are, then we'll find a place away from it all." He winked. "Maybe I can get some kisses."

"If you're a good boy." I laughed and let him lead me away from my comfortable corner. The dogs immediately took our spots. At least we'd have somewhere to sit when we were ready.

Loud voices from outside the kitchen door drew us. Ruthie wouldn't tolerate a fight. I'd have to curb tempers before things got out of hand.

We turned the corner. Sarah was poking the chest of a distinguished man in a tux. "I turned out alright despite your cheating ways and unwillingness to spend one cent of your precious money to help me. I regret the day I ever laid eyes on you."

Ah, the infamous ex-husband, cheater and all-around horrible person. I stepped between them. "What's going on?"

"He came to the kitchen wanting to talk." Sarah crossed her arms. A whiff of alcohol wafted from her breath. "Since I don't want the world knowing my business, we took it outside. Now, tell him to go."

"Sarah…" Robert held out his hands. "I came to apologize."

"Really?" Her eyebrows rose. "Why? Because I now work for one of Hollywood's elite? Aiming to home in on my success?"

He laughed. "You're a cook."

"A mighty fine cook." She two-hand shoved him. "I don't ever want to see you again. I wouldn't shed a tear if you dropped dead. Nor do I care if that floozy you married after you dumped me shares a cent of your money. I don't want anything." Head high, she marched into the house.

He pivoted toward us. "I really did come to apologize."

"Some things can't be resolved. Come on, Mr. Doyles. There's a party happening." I glanced at Sarah, who was watching from the kitchen window as we led him away from the house and toward the pool. A flicker of alarm passed through me about the scent of alcohol on Sarah's breath. Ruthie loved her wine, but she wouldn't tolerate a drunk.

As we neared the area where the majority of the guests mingled, Robert halted. "I need time alone."

"May I ask why it's so important that Sarah speak with you? It didn't seem important enough when she lived on the streets and could have actually used help from you." I narrowed my eyes.

He sighed. "I have some money that belongs to her from a wealthy uncle of hers that died recently. If my wife finds out about it, she'd badger me to give it to her. The woman is draining me dry."

"So, you were hoping Sarah would share this inheritance with you?"

"Of course. If a woman is entitled to half of what a man has after ten years of marriage, why can't it swing the other way? Would you tell her for me? She might listen to you."

I nodded as he strolled toward the rose bushes at

the opposite end of the pool. In a tux, broke and needing money. Such an over-told story.

"I knew it." Sarah hissed from behind a tree. "I knew he'd spill his guts to you, and it had to do with money. He'll not get a penny of what's mine."

"That isn't like you, Sarah." I felt as if I didn't know this bitter woman. The Sarah I knew was kind, loving, and nurturing. "You've been drinking."

"I took a little to get up the nerve to face him." Tears welled in her eyes. "You're right. It isn't me. That man brings out the worst in me." She rushed away.

"Life is never boring around the Canyons," Brock said.

"No, it isn't. Can we go find a place to sit?"

"I'd like nothing better."

We returned to our little alcove. This time, rather than move the dogs, we snuggled onto the lounge chairs with them. Nothing calmed rattled nerves like the unconditional love of an animal.

I must have fallen asleep, completely shirking my hostess duties, because when I opened my eyes, Ruthie stared down at me. "It's three a.m. You completely missed the party. Everyone noticed. There must be a hundred cell-phone photos of you sleeping."

I stretched. "I'm sorry. I didn't realize how tired I was." I glanced to where Brock slept and smiled. He looked so boyish when he was asleep. "I only intended to hide away for a little while. How was the party?"

"A complete success." She grinned. "Everyone

had a good time. We even had some skinny-dipping. I was about to change and take a dip myself to soothe away the pain in my feet from these shoes."

"That sounds like a great idea."

Fifteen minutes later, wearing my favorite navy-blue suit, I raced for the pool's edge and skidded to a halt. Robert Doyles floated facedown among the magnolia blossoms.

Chapter Two

"Call Lori." I sighed. Ruthie might be right about us not being targets, but couldn't we attend a social gathering once without someone being killed? The knife in Robert's back told me he hadn't had too much to drink and drowned.

"That's one of my new kitchen knives." Ruthie glanced from me to Brock.

Brock pulled a cell phone from inside his tux. "I'll place the call." He sounded weary.

I hoped the multitude of deaths that happened around my family didn't make him run away screaming someday. I dashed into the house and grabbed my Kodak. Taking photos of the body wasn't the type of pictures I preferred snapping, but it was the only way I'd have evidence. I'd learned from prior experience that every death that occurred around me linked in some way to my father's murder.

A sleepy-eyed Lori arrived twenty minutes later. "The nights I get a good sleep without you calling are rare, Kelly."

I shrugged one shoulder. "It's a curse, what can I say?" She tolerated a lot from me, considering she'd been in love with my dad when he was killed. Now, we worked together to find his killer. She struggled to keep me at arm's length when she had a case to solve. "How do you think his death is connected to Dad?"

She shot me a sharp look. "Who says it is?"

Another shrug. "Everything seems to be."

"Hold your wild thoughts until we process this." She glanced around, her gaze not staying long on the body. "I'll need your guest list, hired help—you know the drill. Anyone have an argument with the victim?"

I glanced at Ruthie.

"Well?" Lori narrowed her eyes.

"Sarah did, but she didn't kill him."

"Your chef? Bring her out here."

I headed for the guest house on the far side of the property and knocked. The door swung open. Passed out on the couch, a bottle of empty wine clutched in her hands, Sarah snored lightly. I shook her rather hard until her eyes fluttered open.

"It's morning already?"

"It's after three. You need to come with me." I frowned.

"Are you firing me? I swear I'll get sober again." Tears welled in her eyes.

"I'm not firing you. Come on." I took the bottle from her and set it on the glass-topped coffee table.

"Gather your wits about you because it won't be pretty."

She groaned and pushed to her feet. "I'm ready to face the consequences."

If she only knew. I led her to the pool, relieved her gaze didn't immediately flick to the body floating face down in the pool, illuminated by the underwater lights. My own gaze wasn't quite so controlled. My eyes widened to see a magnolia flower plastered to the back of Robert's head.

Lori whipped open a small notebook. "Do you know the man in the water?"

"Huh?" Sarah turned. Her eyes widened, her mouth opened, and she screamed, "Robert."

"Okay, so you know him. What relation are you to him?"

"He's my ex-husband." She sagged to the pool deck. "Why is he still in there? Someone, take him out." Tears poured down her face.

Lori leaned close to her and sniffed. "Have you been drinking?"

"Yes." Sarah covered her face with her hands. "I had to in order to drum up the courage to speak with him."

"Why?"

"Because he's a horrible man."

"I gather it's safe to say that you didn't care for him."

"I loved him, I just didn't like him." Her wails increased.

Jason Banks, my newly-discovered brother and Lori's latest partner in a long line of partners and dirty cops, dead or in jail now, rushed toward us.

"Sorry I'm late. Car wouldn't start. Someone fill me in."

Lori did just that before focusing her attention back to Sarah. "Walk me through your activities of the night. Be as complete as possible."

"I cooked and supervised hired staff for Ruthie's party. After speaking with Robert, I helped clean up and went home to the guest house where I spent the night with a bottle of wine."

"What time?"

"About midnight. I guess there's no way to prove that though."

Ruthie had remained silent through the interview, a rare thing for her. Instead, she sat on a nearby lawn chair and picked at a sequin on her gown.

"Ruthie?" I asked.

"It's bound to come out sooner or later." She took a deep breath. "Sarah wasn't the only one to have an argument with the deceased. He threatened to stop backing our show. But I didn't kill him. I just…slapped him."

"You assaulted him?" Jason's eyes widened.

"If you want to call it that. He was very much alive when I left him standing right where you are."

A muscle ticked in Brock's jaw. I so wanted to ask him what thoughts went through his mind.

He moved to the side of the pool and stared at the body. "Has anyone noticed anything weird about the body?"

Jason stepped up next to him. "There's no blood." He peered closer, then jumped into the pool and turned the body over. "Seriously, dude."

Robert blinked, breathing out of a small mouth apparatus with a tube tiny enough to hide behind his ear. He spit out the mouthpiece and swam to the side of the pool.

"You idiot. What were you thinking? Did you think we'd ignore a dead body in the pool and not call the police? How could you pretend such a thing?" Sarah reached over and slapped him.

He shrugged. "My mounting debt has me doing crazy things. I didn't think it through. I just wanted out."

"Insurance fraud is a felony. You could get ten years." Lori said.

"Then call it insanity."

"Hard to prove. You're not insane. You're just stupid."

"Idiot." Sarah said again before she shoved him back into the water.

"Ma'am, you'll have to keep your hands to yourself, or I'll haul you to jail for assault." Lori crossed her arms. "This is the most ridiculous call I've ever been on. I cannot believe I didn't look close enough to see he was still breathing. That's what happens when you get too used to being called to the same destination." She glared at me. "You know enough about crime scenes by this time, Kelly."

"You were half asleep when you got here." I glared at Robert. "How did you plan on fooling ME?"

"You should have just gone away." Sarah lunged to her feet. "Much as I'd like him to be locked up for the next ten, can't you pretend he was just snorkeling? Nobody's hurt. Nobody's dead."

"Sit down, ma'am." Jason said, shaking his head. "Anyone want to press charges here? If not, I'm going home to bed."

"Can I press charges for someone scaring me half to death?" Ruthie asked. "I seriously thought I was going to be a murder suspect. I'd rather leave that thrill to Kelly."

Lori looked ready to pull her hair out. "Next time you find a body, check to make sure it's dead. Take note. I will arrest you if you pull anything like this again."

I grinned. "You always tell me not to touch." Relief flooded through me. I didn't want another murder investigation hanging over my head. It took time away from finding out who killed my father. Not that I had much to go on. The trail of clues he'd left me had grown cold.

"False alarm," Lori told the arriving paramedics as she strode toward the gate.

After she and Jason left, I glanced around at the others. "You can go, Robert. I suggest you not pay us a visit again."

He nodded. "Sorry, ladies. I'll have to think of something else. Ruthie, I don't have the funding to back your show. I'm sorry." He put a hand to his reddened cheek and shuffled away.

"Life is never boring around here." Brock sat on the chair where the knife lay.

"What made you take a closer look?" Ruthie asked. "Couldn't the water have washed away the blood?"

"Not that much of it. While the rest of you were

talking, I was trying to think of a way to keep Sarah from being locked up. Robert really did her wrong during their divorce. She has plenty of reasons to hate him." He glanced up with a smile. "So, I looked at Robert instead. It helps me focus to stare at something. Anyway, I thought I saw his head turn once when Sarah cried."

"My investigative hero." I removed the knife from the seat and dropped down next to him. "I guess you aren't tired of all the chaos swirling around me all the time."

"Never. It keeps me on my toes." He rested an arm around my shoulders and gave me a quick hug. "I'm beat, so I'll head home. Where's Morgan by the way?"

"I had a fight with him, too," Ruthie said. She exhaled heavily. "I told him I wanted to get married, and he ran away like I'd caught him stealing a cookie."

"He didn't say anything?" My eyebrows rose.

"Nope. Just turned tail and ran." She stood and smoothed her gown. "Guess that's that." Shoulders squared, she scooped up Sassy from where the dog lay at her feet and trudged toward the house.

"He wouldn't break up with her for that, would he?" Sarah stared after Ruthie. "Maybe I should go talk to her. Men can be such scum. Except for you, Brock. You're one of a kind."

"Thank you, I think." Brock chuckled.

"Let her have some time to herself," I said. "Morgan will be back. He's crazy about her. I bet he'll come back with a ring."

The way Brock paled informed me I was right.

My boyfriend knew a secret. "Okay, spill," I said, when Sarah returned to her cottage.

"He told me about Ruthie's proposal. Yes, he took off, probably not the wisest thing to do with no explanation, but he is purchasing a ring."

I laughed. "It had better be a big one. She seems pretty upset."

He helped me to my feet. "I have a feeling he could give her something from the dollar store and she'd be happy."

"You're right." I stretched up on my toes to kiss him. "Thank you for not growing tired of all the drama."

"Drama is my life, Darlin'." He pressed his lips to mine and everything settled back nicely into place.

Chapter Three

The next weekend, I wore a gown of black with shimmering threads running through it and strolled the red carpet on Brock's arm. Cameras flashed around us as paparazzi yelled our names. I smiled and waved, posed for photos, and couldn't get inside fast enough. I'd never get used to the attention, and for certain, I'd never relish it like Ruthie did.

She paused and waved every couple of feet while Morgan stood off to the side, fidgeting in the new tux she'd bought him. On her left ring finger sparkled a four-carat diamond ring. The man would be in debt for the rest of his life.

I flashed one more smile and wave before entering the building. It was going to be a long night. Ruthie had already planned another party, smaller this time, thank goodness. Win or lose, she planned to celebrate.

Brock pulled out my chair and I sat at a round table near the stage. Already, the room was filled. I shouldn't have been surprised to see Robert Doyles there, but I was. Not only was he a producer of the show, but the way he kept changing seats, he must have hired on as a seat-filler. The man really must be broke. I felt sorry for him. It had to be a blow to the ego to take what Hollywood would consider a menial job.

"It looks as if he's already had a bit too much to drink," Brock said, following my gaze.

"He's embarrassing himself," Ruthie added, taking her seat next to me. "Go talk to him, Morgan."

"And tell him what?" He frowned.

"To find a place to sit and stop attracting attention." She waved a dismissive hand, the left one, causing the ring to flash under the dimmed lights.

"Nice rock." Robert made a beeline for our table, saving Morgan from having to get up.

"Thank you," Ruthie beamed and held out her hand. "I'm engaged."

"Congratulations. Seems you might have more than one reason to celebrate tonight." He looked like a bear eying a bush full of juicy berries.

I made eye contact with Brock and mouthed, "Watch him closely tonight."

Brock nodded. "You feeling okay, Robert?"

"Never better, but it is a bit hot in here, don't you think?" He tugged at his tie.

"I thought it chilly." I narrowed my eyes. The man sweated through his jacket. His face as red as a glass of merlot. "I think you should stay seated for a while." He seriously looked ill.

We quieted as the emcee took the stage. Eric James Johnson III, hosted tonight's event. As the new owner, having recently inheriting the studio, he insisted it be his first duty. I wasn't sure what that had to do anything, since the man was as boring as a tomato, but who was I to argue?

After almost two hours, I suddenly straightened as Iris Beacon, one of Hollywood's elite from an earlier era, approached the microphone. She'd announce the winner of our category. On the screen behind her flashed videos of the shows competing.

Ruthie squealed and clapped as our faces flashed across the big screen. "This is so exciting." Even I had a hard time holding down the excitement bubbling in me. I gripped Brock's hand and waited for the announcement.

Iris opened a black envelope. "The winner is...*The Hart of Crime*." She smiled in our direction.

Gripping Ruthie's arm to keep her from bolting up the steps without me, we walked at a leisurely pace, my heart threatening to burst free. We won. I couldn't believe it.

"Thank you." Ruthie held the trophy high. "There is no greater pleasure than acting in a winning show, but working with my granddaughter, Kelly, is the second greatest honor." She smiled at me.

Tears stung my eyes. Not only had she publicly announced that she was my grandmother, something she forbade me to disclose because she said it aged her, but she seemed to consider acting alongside me as an honor. She stepped back to let me talk.

I stepped up to the microphone and peered across the crowd of faces. "Once upon a time, there was a little girl who wanted to be an investigative journalist. Then, life threw her a curve ball and she got roped into acting. Oh, I've grumbled and fussed about my new role, but I'm right where I'm supposed to be." I put an arm around Ruthie's shoulders. "Playing at working right alongside my best friend. I love you, Grandma." Amidst claps and cheers, I placed a kiss on Ruthie's cheek.

We were two teary-eyed winners as we made our way back to our seats. I cast a quick glance at Robert's empty chair and hoped he hadn't missed as a result of his financial backing. If he had money problems, then our show had contributed.

After the ceremony, we gathered with twenty of Ruthie's closest friends in the industry for a buffet, champagne, and celebration. I'd meant the words of my speech. Though reluctant to enter the world of acting, I'd grown to love the occupation despite myself, although I'd prefer to do so without public attention every time I left the house.

"You did good, baby." Brock leaned over and kissed my forehead.

"This has been one of the best days of my life." I wished Dad could have been there to see.

Robert staggered past us, a flute of champagne in his hand. Brock made a move to stop him, but Morgan beat him to it.

"Come on, man. Sit." Morgan shoved him into a

chair and took away his drink. "Someone, fetch him some coffee."

"I'm not feeling well." Robert put a hand to his throat. "It's blasted hot in here."

"I think there's something wrong with him." I studied his clammy face. "Do we need to call an ambulance?"

Robert's eyes widened, and he keeled over. With my heart in my throat, I felt for a pulse. "Too late for that. We need to call the police. He isn't faking this time."

Morgan cleared the room, sending the party guests back to the theater. "I called Lori," he said when he returned. "She cussed me out and said she'd be here in ten minutes. Wasn't far away, considering how things always go wrong when someone's up for an award or throwing a party."

"Not always." Ruthie plopped into a chair. "Just a lot. There's a difference."

"Tell her that." He sat next to her.

The four of us sat silent until Lori and Jason arrived. I watched as they examined the body before taking it for granted he was dead. Then, Lori whirled to face us.

"Kelly, tell me what happened." Lori whipped out her notebook, leaving Jason to contain the scene.

"I'm not sure." My brow furrowed. "He'd been drinking a lot and complained about being hot for the last few hours. Then, he fell over."

I glanced up at the snap of a camera. Susan Gilroy, reporter for the *Hollywood Tribune*, ducked behind one of the buffet tables. Sneaky woman. She must have hidden behind the tablecloth when Morgan cleared the room.

"Out, Miss Gilroy," Lori ordered. "No reporters. Wait for our statement like everyone else."

"Come on, Detective. I'm here. Let me get a story."

"Out." Lori pointed.

Susan pouted and left, Morgan closing the door after her. "That woman's a nuisance."

I agreed, and we didn't like each other much, but since I used to be the main photographer for *The Tribune*, I understood her thirst for a story. "It was clever of her to hide. You should let her have first scoop."

Lori sighed. "Okay. Hot, sweaty, stumbling, now dead, taking place over the course of a few hours."

"Heart attack?" Brock suggested.

"Poison?" I asked.

"Well, something killed him, whether natural or not." Lori snapped her notebook closed. "I really wish you Canyon women could stay out of trouble. I've other things to concentrate on." Her gaze fell on Robert. "I guess he found a way to escape his financial woes after all."

"And leave his wife a wealthy widow if he had good life insurance," Ruthie said. "She's my number-one suspect."

"You and Kelly will stay out of this." Lori's canned response didn't sound convincing. She knew us too well.

Ruthie shook her head. "Solving crime helps my acting. It gives me realism."

Lori paled. "I hope I never find out you stage these murders to help your acting career."

"Of course not, but I don't turn down an opportunity to improve my craft." Ruthie crossed her arms and pouted.

I rolled my eyes. "You aren't helping. Isn't the main thing here a man is dead? Whether he was well-liked or not, leaving behind a rich widow, helping your career…none of it matters except that he is dead."

"Thank you." Lori nodded in my direction. "Let's get this matter settled for the night, the body to the morgue, and statements taken. I need the four of you to go to separate corners of the room. I'll get to you when I can."

The others scattered, Ruthie hugging the trophy like it was a teddy bear. I stayed put and toed off my stilettos. Ruthie was right about one thing. Robert left behind a very young, very wealthy widow, which put her at the top of my suspect list, too. I could placate Lori until Christmas, but I wouldn't be able to not investigate. It was like a drug, solving a murder.

I slyly retrieved my cell phone from my sparkly clutch and snapped a few photos of the body. Not as good of quality as my Kodak, but the device would work in a pinch.

"You shouldn't do that," Jason said behind me.

I shrieked and shoved the phone back into my clutch. "You shouldn't sneak up on people when there's been a murder. I could have shot you."

"With your phone? I doubt your gun would fit in the silly thing." He motioned to the clutch. "I'm here to take your statement."

"Okay, but I've already told you everything I know."

"Tell me again." He wrote down the same things I'd told Lori, which she'd written down. "He was a seat filler? One of those people who covers when someone has to go to the bathroom?"

"I assumed he was because he kept changing seats. Now that I think about it, he might have been filching drinks. He was wasted. Of course, it might have been poison that killed him."

"We don't know that. Don't make assumptions."

"People don't die of natural causes around me."

"True." He shut his notepad and sat down across from me. "Let me talk to you as your brother, not as a police officer."

I nodded. "Go ahead."

"You being a photographer, you see things others don't. I know what you've told me, but what have you seen that you haven't said? Think about it."

I closed my eyes and thought about the guests in attendance. Actors, producers, Louie our director…my eyes snapped open. "Why wasn't Robert's wife here? This was a big deal for his career, broke or not. Wouldn't you think she'd have come with her husband?"

Chapter Four

The next morning, I sat in the chair while Lisa did my makeup for the day's filming. I filled her in on last night's event. Not only did she do a fabulous job getting me ready for work, but she was nothing short of a computer genius and had a keen mind for research.

"I heard Lana Doyles was at a retreat." She made quote marks with her fingers. "You don't think she got those boobs naturally, do you? Word is she's having her nose and lips done."

"Why? Isn't she like twenty-five?" I glanced up, getting my hair pulled for my effort. More importantly, how could she afford the expense if Robert was broke?

"More like thirty-five. Sit still. I need you to look roughed up, but still pretty."

"When did she leave?"

"Sometime yesterday, so she would still have

had time to poison her husband, if he died that way." She almost choked me with a cloud of hair spray. "Word is her appointment was last night, scheduled under the cover of darkness. As if no one will be able to tell."

"True. They haven't ruled out a heart attack." I glanced in the mirror. Tousled hair, artfully applied bruises…yep, I looked like I'd been in a fight, yet still resembled the pretty girl next door the director wanted me to be. "When does she get back?"

Lisa shrugged. "I'm not into the whole body modification thing. I have no idea how long it takes. With her husband dead, I'm guessing she'll be back soon, right?"

Hmmm. I'd have to plan a trip to pay my condolences to the widow and do some snooping at the same time. "See what you can dig up on her and Robert, okay?"

She nodded. "Not only is she having work done, but she's hired an interior decorator to go along with the housekeeper and chef already on staff." Lisa stepped back and smiled. "There. You're ready to run around the set."

"You're a marvel." I grabbed my backpack and raced out the door. As usual, I'd spent too much time talking and arrived a few minutes late.

Louie glared. "Glad you could join us."

"Sorry." I plopped my bag in a corner and followed the cast behind the studio where a set-up alley waited. Today's shoot picked up where the last had ended. With me beaten and dumped in a pile of garbage, left for dead, and my "mother," played by Ruthie, out of this scene because she's searching for me. Except Kelly Hart never died. She sought justice with a gun and her badge.

To pay me back for being late, Louie had us redo the take over and over and over. By the time lunch rolled around, I really did feel as if I'd been beaten up. I headed for the cafeteria to have lunch with Brock.

"Rough morning?" His eyes widened as his gaze traveled from head to my feet.

"I was late again."

"Ah. I ordered your favorite." He motioned to the chicken salad sandwich and kettle chips.

"Thanks, but you know I like burgers with bacon." I smiled.

"They were out. This is pretty much all they had." He gave an apologetic shrug.

"I'm hungry enough to eat almost anything." I bit into the sandwich. Not bad. Good, actually. As we ate, I told Brock about my conversation with Lisa.

"Lana is a wannabe star." He wiped his mouth on a napkin. "She's had a few bit parts but has absolutely no talent. So, marrying a rich man was the next best thing."

"Except Robert is no longer rich."

"I doubt he told her. He always treated Lana as a trophy wife."

"But she could have found out."

He nodded. "Yep, which would give her a motive for murder. Her husband is worth more dead than alive."

Ruthie rushed to our table and plopped down on an empty chair. "Guess what I learned about Lana

Doyles?”

“That’s she’s having plastic surgery?”

“Darn. How do you always beat me to the information?” She crossed her arms and pouted. “I bet you don’t know which retreat she’s at.”

“No, I don’t.” I grinned. “Where?”

“Someplace in Tucson.”

“Oh.” My shoulders slumped. I didn’t have the time to make a drive that far away.

“But…” Ruthie held up a hand. “She’s coming home tonight because of her husband’s death.” She looked quite pleased with herself. “I offered to pick her up from the airport so as to keep her and her bandages out of the public’s view.”

“It’s scary how your mind works,” Brock said.

“Thank you.” Ruthie’s grin widened. “We leave right after you finish shooting. But Louie said it would be a long day.”

Great. A quick glance at the clock on the wall had me sprinting for the set.

Louie hadn’t lied about a long day. We shot two more scenes before he let us go. At eight p.m., I slid behind the wheel of my 1970 Aqua-colored Camaro convertible and picked Ruthie up from home before speeding to the airport where Lana would be waiting in the parking garage.

We drove past a woman in a faded red hoodie twice before Ruthie recognized her. “There.”

I stopped the car.

“Put the top up,” Lana hissed, climbing into the backseat. “I can’t be recognized.” She removed her hoodie revealing two black eyes, a bandaged nose, and swollen lips. Her platinum-white hair shone like a beacon. *Oh, I get it. She's trying to look like Marilyn Monroe.*

She looked so much like a puffer fish I had to turn away to keep from laughing. I put the top up and pulled from the garage, following her directions like an obedient cab driver.

"I'm, uh, sorry for your loss?" I peered in the rearview mirror.

"Thanks." She stared out the window, but not before I saw the shimmer of tears in her eyes. Tears of loss or guilt?

She lived in a mansion in Beverly Hills. Using a remote, she opened the iron gates and I drove up a winding drive to a stylish one-story that had to be at least five-thousand square feet. Modest by Hollywood standards.

"Thank you for the ride." She shoved open her door. "Would you like to come in for coffee?"

"Yes," Ruthie and I said in unison.

I think Lana might have tried to raise her eyebrows, but her face didn't move. Instead, she nodded and headed for the front door.

It opened before she reached the top step. A woman in a dark dress and white collar stepped aside for us to enter. "Welcome home, Mrs. Doyles. My condolences on the loss of your husband."

"Thank you, Mildred." Lana removed her outer clothing and handed them to the woman. "Burn these. I bought them for a good price from a homeless person. Please inform Cheryl to prepare coffee and cake. We have guests."

Mildred nodded and turned down a marble-tiled hall.

The home was decorated in white. Everywhere. A few ice-blue throw pillows and a faux-zebra rug the only breaks in the starkness. "Nice place," I said.

"Thank you. It won't be the same now. Maybe I should redecorate in shades of something dark for mourning." She flopped onto a chaise longue and pulled a fur throw over her. She stared at us for a moment. "Well, sit down."

We perched on the edge of a sofa in uncomfortable silence until Mildred returned with a silver tray filled with tiny cakes, a carafe, and three mugs. She set it on a glass-topped coffee table. "Cheryl wants to know if she can retire to her room?"

Lana waved a dismissive hand. "You may go, too." She muttered something unflattering about Cheryl, then glanced up at us with a sad smile. "Ruthie, would you pour? My heart has me feeling rather weak."

"Of course." Ruthie poured us each a cup of coffee. "I get the impression you aren't fond of your chef? I have confrontations with my own on occasion, but she's great at her job. Chefs can be rather temperamental."

Lana sneered, I thought. Hard to tell with a face that stayed in a bland expression. "She has a lot to learn. Robert hired her, I didn't. He always had a soft heart for a pretty face and a sob story." She stabbed us with a sharp gaze. "I know you're full of questions, so ask."

"Why do you think that?" I sipped at the rather bitter drink, then added a heavy dose of cream from a small pitcher.

"Because everyone knows how nosy the two of you are. Fine. I'll begin. I suppose you want to know about my marriage?" She lifted her chin.

"Sure." I smiled to cover a grimace. The coffee wasn't improved by cream.

"I did my thing, and Robert did his, usually with someone else."

"He had a mistress?" Ruthie perked up. "You mean he did the same thing to you that—" She clapped a hand over her mouth.

"That he did to Sarah? Not exactly. I didn't leave in a snit, and thus, have no money. I'm smarter than that." She chewed the cuticle of her thumb, then sat on her hand. "Bad habits are hard to break."

Out of the corner of my eye, I caught a glimpse of a pretty little brunette in a chef's hat and jacket. If looks could kill, Lana would be toast. Cheryl curled her lip and ducked through a side door. I put her down on my next-to-be-questioned list.

"Perhaps Robert got kinder," I suggested, setting my mug back on the tray. "He did show up to talk to Sarah. He seemed apologetic."

She looked surprised at the news. "I doubt it. We've had our rows over it all. I decided that as long as I can do what I want and buy what makes me happy, then I don't care what he does." The new tears forming in her eyes told a different story.

"Do you mind if I ask who his girlfriend is?"

"You mean girlfriends. You saw one walk out the door, if I'm not mistaken. Oh, they've tried to be discreet, but I've caught them sharing more than ice cream late at night. Mildred's the only woman I don't worry about him cheating with." She heaved a heavy sigh. "I know there are others, but I don't know their names."

The doorbell rang, and Mildred glided past us. I'd almost forgotten she was there, especially since Lana had dismissed her. Curious why she'd stayed. To listen in on our conversation? Lana didn't seem to mind speaking of the dirt in her marriage in front of the housekeeper. I turned to see a red-face Lori and Jason enter.

"We gave her a ride," Ruthie said. "Because we're nice. Not because we're snooping."

Lori rolled her eyes. "I'm sorry for your loss, Mrs. Doyles. Mind if we ask you a few questions?" She gave me a pointed look.

"Fine. We were just leaving." I grabbed a cake, took a bite, and spit the sawdust-tasting thing into a napkin. Yep, Cheryl had a lot to learn.

"Do you think it's worth hiding out here and asking Jason whether he learned anything we don't know?" Ruthie's teeth shone under the moonlight.

"No." I marched for the car. "Lori and Jason knew we were here as soon as they drove up."

"Oh, right. The Aqua Machine gave us away." She slid into the passenger seat. "Want to go hunt up Cheryl?"

"Yes, but not tonight. It's almost midnight, and we have to shoot tomorrow. I'm exhausted."

"Be on the set on time, and Louie won't take his frustration out on you." She grinned.

I tried. I really did.

When we returned home, and I'd climbed into

bed with Shutterbug at my side, I booted up my laptop to see an email from Lisa.

"Get to work a half hour early in the morning. I've got some dirt."

I smiled, closed my laptop, and curled under the blankets. I wouldn't be late in the morning.

Chapter Five

"Okay, girlfriend. Spill." I plopped into the makeup chair while Ruthie took a place on the sofa.

"Robert is in debt to some bad people. He has a weakness for Las Vegas and everything that goes with it." Lisa's hand shook as she applied foundation to my face. "I think you should stay out of this one, Kelly. You don't want to mess with the mob."

She's right, I didn't. "I'm not afraid of Vegas. What are you not telling me?"

"Lana was seen recently having dinner with Martin Rossi."

"So…"

"He's one of the top people in the mob. Really, Kelly, you need to keep up on current events." Ruthie slapped down the magazine she'd been flipping through. "These guys are like the Sopranos and Marlon Brando. Very dangerous. Are we going to Vegas?"

"No." I narrowed my eyes. I agreed with Lisa. "We're staying out of this one."

"Okay, but your dad had a few run-ins with Rossi. There might be information there. We've come this far, why run off scared now?"

"I like my head where it is, not in the trunk of the Aqua Machine!" It did make sense, kind of. If Dad had gotten on the wrong side of the mob…well, it could explain a lot of things. Like his murder, for one. The last few months proved that he knew something he shouldn't have known and was trying to bring it into the open. Still, I wanted to do some more digging before committing to a trip to Vegas.

"Stop being so dramatic. I thought you wanted to solve your father's murder. I guess I was mistaken." She stormed from the trailer.

"I do," I whispered.

Lisa patted my shoulder. "I want to go with you when you go."

Was I that transparent? I sighed. "I can't go anywhere for a few weeks." Unless we made it a weekend trip, which wouldn't leave much time if we found a trail of clues to follow. In the meantime, I could see what I could find out about Lana's dinner with Rossi.

Ruthie yanked open the door to the trailer. "Are you done yet? I don't want to be late. I have dinner with Morgan to plan our wedding." Slam.

I sighed. "Guess I should tell her we're going to Vegas." I'd do almost anything to defuse the Ruthie grenade. "I'll let you know when. We still have filming to do. If we're going, I'd prefer it not be a one-day trip."

"Good point." Lisa nodded. "No reason to have the mob follow you home."

Now, there was a cheery thought. I removed the plastic bib and rushed out of the trailer. Ruthie stood, arms crossed, outside the door. "You film first today. Tell Louie I'll be there in time for my scene." She glared and stormed inside.

I guess I should have told her then we'd go to the City of Sin, but with her throwing such a childish tantrum, a bit of torture was in order. Smiling, I headed for the studio. Today's scene was indoors in the "precinct."

"What's so humorous?" Louie glanced up from his chair. "Proud because you actually made it on time?"

"Think what you want." My smile widened. "I'm here, and Ruthie will be soon. What are you waiting for?"

"Mouthy actors." Louie snapped his fingers, and the filming started.

Ruthie arrived a few minutes before her lines. Mild days of filming involved little more than memorizing lines, something that came easy to me. When we'd finished for the day, I didn't feel as if I'd worked at all.

Since removing the makeup didn't take much more than half a dozen makeup-remover wipes, Lisa left early. I entered the silent trailer and sighed. Quiet until Ruthie caught up with me, anyway. One, two…

"What a day!" The trailer door slammed open. "I can't believe I fumbled my lines."

"One word, Ruthie. You did fine." I faced her, noting the sadness in her eyes. "What's wrong?"

"What makes you think anything is wrong?" She brushed past me and grabbed a wipe.

"You look tired, and you've been as grumpy as a feral cat." I set to work on my face.

Tears welled in her eyes. "Do you think I'm too old to have a big wedding? Maybe Morgan and I should just elope. Maybe get married in Vegas."

I frowned. "Is this a ploy to investigate the news Lisa gave us, because I've already decided to go once we're finished filming this season."

"Not completely." She plopped onto the sofa. "I'm in my mid-fifties, Kelly. Oh, I know I look younger, and makeup helps even more, but…" She shrugged.

More like late fifties, but I'd let that subject slide. I took her hands in mine. "You'd like the wedding you've always wanted. Because you didn't get one with Grandpa, right?"

"Yup, we went to the courthouse." She straightened. "You're right. I'm going to have the wedding of my dreams and have the ceremony and reception on our back lawn. This time I'll let you be the photographer…after the ceremony. I want you to stand up with me. Oh, and I want you to take our engagement photos."

"Thank you. I'm honored." I grinned.

She waved her hand at me. "You're my best friend. Who else would I choose?" She rubbed her hands together and resumed removing her makeup.

"What's next on finding who killed Robert?"

Sometimes I got dizzy from the way she flitted from one subject to the next. "I'd like to talk to the chef, and his widow again about her dinner with Rossi, and take it from there. Maybe that will give us more information before we hit the streets of Vegas."

"Do you wonder why in the world we bother to get involved? I mean, Lori and Jason are capable law enforcement officers."

"I know why I do." I swallowed past the lump in my throat. "Because when I was a suspect in Lauren's death, we saw signs of Dad knowing too much about someone. Then there was Lori's dirty partner and the corrupt studio owner...I simply want justice. Even if we don't find out who killed Dad, it helps me to bring justice to other unlawful deaths. Does that make sense?"

"It does to me." She scooted over so I could see in the mirror.

My mind raced as I scrubbed my forehead. Where would we find Robert's chef/girlfriend? We couldn't very well knock on Lana's door and ask her. I suppose we could ask her about her meeting with Rossi, then slip away to question Cheryl. Felt risky, but might be doable. Ruthie was the queen of distractions. Or I could ask Jason to give me her address...no, he wouldn't.

"Hello to the two most beautiful women I know." Brock entered the trailer. After tossing Ruthie a wink, he planted a kiss behind my right ear. He knew exactly how to make me melt.

I hummed and smiled. "Hello to you too, Mr.

Handsome."

He chuckled. "What are you up to today?"

"I'm having dinner with Morgan." Ruthie smiled at the mirror. "Then, we were going to question the cute little chef with loose morals who works for Lana."

His brow furrowed. "Didn't you already pay Lana a visit?"

"Yes," I said, "but new information has come up. I'll fill you in during dinner." I turned my attention to Ruthie. "Visiting Lana will have to wait until tomorrow. By the time you and Morgan are finished, it'll be too late."

She pouted. "Fine. Bye." She sailed out the door.

"Don't worry about her attitude. She thinks she's too old to get married."

"That's ridiculous."

"I know, but you know how high-strung she is." I smiled up at him. "Want to go to Staletti's for dinner?"

"That sounds great." His arm snaked around my waist and he pulled me in for a proper kiss. Fifteen minutes later, we headed for the Aqua Machine.

Brock had several cars, a Porsche, a Mercedes, and a beat-up old Ford truck, but he loved driving the Camaro, and I enjoyed watching the pleasure on his face as he sat in the driver's seat. He's the only one I let drive Ruthie's old car, a gift to me a few months ago since she didn't like driving.

"Uh-oh," I said, spotting Morgan's car in Staletti's parking lot. "They'll think we're homing in on their wedding planning."

"We'll ask to be seated in the tea room. It shouldn't be a problem."

Of course, that's exactly where Ruthie and Morgan were seated. The look on my grandmother's face as we entered almost made me turn tail and run. Instead, I asked the hostess to seat us as far from them as the intimate room would allow.

The table she led us to nestled against a window overlooking a fountain and flower garden. The round table, decked out with a starched white tablecloth, hurricane lamp, and a silk rose, was the perfect spot for a romantic dinner for two. Leo Staletti prided himself on ambiance, but didn't require a dress code, thus making this my favorite restaurant.

The man himself approached our table. "Hello, you two. Why aren't you sitting with them?" He jerked his thumb toward Ruthie's table.

"They're planning their wedding and don't want us around." I smiled.

"She'd better be planning on letting us cater the event." He laid a hand on his chest. "Almost broke my heart when she didn't hire us for her party."

"I'm sure she will, but it wouldn't hurt to drop some subtle hints in her direction."

He pulled a brochure from inside his apron pocket and headed over to drop it on Ruthie's table. "I expect to be hired this time," he said loud enough for the room to hear. With a nod in my direction, he headed for the kitchen.

I laughed at Ruthie's shocked expression. So much for subtlety.

After placing our orders, I filled Brock in on last night's visit to Lana. "She seemed sad, but I wasn't sure whether it was because of Robert's infidelity with Cheryl or his death. Lana's hard to read with her face swollen from plastic surgery."

"Did you know Robert met her when she posed as Marilyn Monroe on the Hollywood Walk of Fame?" he asked. "Now, she's determined to look exactly like the icon."

"Sad."

"Yeah, she was pretty enough before getting the work done." He sat back and crossed his arms. "Are you really going to look into Martin Rossi?"

"Maybe." I tilted my head. "I'd like to talk to Lana again first, though. Do you know her?"

"Only in passing. Do you want me to go with you?"

"Besides Ruthie, you're the best distraction when a woman is involved." I grinned. Most women couldn't resist his charm and good looks. I'd learned early on in our relationship that jealousy played no part with us. Brock loved me and was as faithful as a Bassett Hound.

"We're going back tomorrow night."

"Great. I'm free and can't turn down an opportunity for adventure with the Canyon women. Unless it involves a whorehouse again. That was unpleasant."

I laughed, drawing the attention of nearby diners. "I promise, you won't be put in any uncompromising positions." Thank goodness, the girl he'd interviewed let him ask questions, willing to sit and talk for her money instead of the alternative. Brock had gone on to save her from that life, so the minor tarnish of his halo had been polished.

"Did you learn to shoot the gun you bought?"

I curled my lips. "Yes, and I'm not a bad shot. I still don't like the gun and would rather use the stun gun or pepper spray."

"If you're going to start asking questions about Rossi, then carry the gun." His look broached no argument.

Twenty-five years old, and I still let people tell me what to do. I sighed and dug into my lasagna.

Brock put his hand over mine. "Don't be mad. I just don't want you to get killed, and the way you stick your pretty little nose into troublesome places—"

"I know." I'd come close to joining my father in heaven on more than one occasion. If Lori found out I was packing, she'd have a heart attack and find a reason to lock me up for my own safety.

Chapter Six

The next evening, we parked the Aqua Machine in front of Lana's house. Ruthie peered over the front seat. "It doesn't look like anyone's home."

"I'm checking the garage." I shoved open my door, scooting out of the car before Brock could stop me, and headed for the massive garage to the right and back of the mansion. I didn't believe for a second Lana had left the house so soon after surgery.

I cupped my hands around my eyes and waited for them to focus through the murkiness. A small light burned in a far corner. Motion sensor. I hoped there wasn't a security camera, just in case I had to let myself in. Three cars sat inside, a Mercedes, a Jeep, and a foreign make I wasn't familiar with. Somebody had to be home.

I waved the others forward and climbed the

three steps to the front door. "Somebody has to be here. There's a light on in the garage."

Morgan scowled. "Security lights mean nothing."

"We can at least check." Ruthie peeked through a small slit in the front window blinds. "I see movement." She pressed the doorbell.

Mildred might have gone home for the night, it being seven, but she'd stayed late the last time we were there. I got the impression she was not only a housekeeper, but a companion of sorts. Morgan reached around me and rapped his knuckles on the wood.

The door eased open. "Who is it?" Lana whispered. "I've a migraine."

I stepped back and ushered Brock forward. No headache in the world could resist him.

Lana was no different. "Oh." She opened the door further, tightening the belt of her robe, which did nothing more than expose the low-cut bodice of her silk nightgown. "Come in, please."

"I asked Kelly to bring me by to pay my respects." He smiled down at her. Only a flicker in his eyes showed his surprise at the bruises on her face and the bandage across her nose.

Wait a minute. She had more bruises than the night before. One on her cheek looked fresh. She might have had surgery, but someone else had tried to inflict damage to her already-tortured face. "Did someone hit you?"

She stumbled back. "No, I've had work done. You know that."

Okay. I'd let her lie go for now, but soon she'd

have to tell me who beat her.

"Yes, let's sit." Brock tucked her hand in the crook of his arm and led her to the chaise longue. "You must be exhausted."

"It has been a rather tiring week." She fluttered her eyelashes at him seconds before she bellowed, "Mildred!"

"Yes, Mrs. Doyles. I'm way ahead of you." The housekeeper set a tray of coffee and cookies on the table. "I'll be right over here if you need anything more." She cut a quick glance at Morgan and paled. "Mark?"

Ruthie's eyes widened. "You know each other?"

Morgan nodded. "We were neighbors growing up." He smiled. "We played many a game of red rover and freeze tag together." He clasped his hands around hers. "It's good to see you again, Millie."

Lana cleared her throat, preventing the other woman from saying anything. "You may go home, Mildred. I can handle things here." She clearly didn't like a man's attention on any woman but her. Once Mildred left, she focused her hungry eyes on Brock.

My fingers curled. Lay one scarlet-tipped nail on him, and…

Brock sat next to her and laid a hand on hers. "You can be honest with us, Ms. Doyles—"

"Please call me Lana." More eye fluttering.

"Lana." His soft voice seemed to make the woman turn to butter. "I need you to be honest with us. The bruise on your cheekbone has nothing to do with your surgery. Who hit you? I want to make sure you're safe."

"Was it Martin Rossi?" I asked.

Her head whipped around. "Where did you hear that name?"

"I've got sources."

"You're a busybody, Kelly Canyon. You do not want to get involved in this." Her gaze flicked to where Mildred had gone.

Question answered. She did have involvement, and either Mildred knew, or she didn't want to say too much in front of the woman. "Maybe you should hire a bodyguard."

She glanced at Morgan and smiled. "How much?"

"Not on your life." Ruthie glared. "He's my bodyguard."

Morgan's lips twitched. "I can recommend someone to you, if you're serious." He knelt next to the lounge chair. "Why did he hit you?"

"He didn't. One of his goons did." She twisted her robe in her hands. "Robert owes him a lot of money. I made Rossi a proposition to pay back my husband's gambling debts. He accepted. I'm his now, and he can do anything he wants, so a bodyguard would only be killed. Thanks for the offer."

"Could you go into hiding?" Morgan asked. "Take a vacation somewhere quiet where no one would expect you to be."

"No." She sighed. "Let's not talk about this anymore. I'm not sure if I can trust my hired help. I'm sure Rossi has spies everywhere."

Speaking of spies. I caught a glimpse of Cheryl peeking from the kitchen. On the pretense of needing to use the restroom, I headed in her direction.

She caught sight of me coming and busied herself digging around in an industrial-size refrigerator. After clearing my throat several times, I tapped her on the shoulder.

"Go away. You'll get me fired. I'm supposed to be invisible to guests."

"If you haven't been fired by now, my asking you questions isn't going to hurt anything."

She straightened and faced me. "What do you want?"

"You don't seem distraught for someone intimately involved with Robert Doyles." I narrowed my eyes.

"It isn't my place to be distraught. You don't know how I am in the privacy of my own home." She set a stick of butter on the counter next to a small marble mortar and pestle. "I made fresh bread. Would you like a slice?"

Remembering the other things I'd tasted by her hands, I shook my head. "Any idea who might have killed him?"

"If it was someone in this house, it would be Lana. She's got a temper."

Hmmm. His murder didn't seem like a spur-of-the-moment thing. He'd been acting funny for a few hours. I needed to ask Lori how he died. My guess...poison. Who better to use that weapon than a chef?

"Or it could have been Mildred," Cheryl said. "She'll do almost anything for her highness. Then you have Rossi. Actually, there is quite a list of people wanting my Robert out of the picture." Her voice cracked a bit. "But, it wasn't me." She added a few apricots to the assorted ingredients on the counter. "I'm probably the only person in this city who loved him."

Maybe. I hurried to the bathroom before someone caught me in my lie. Flushed the toilet, ran water in the sink, and snooped through the medicine cabinet. Viagra, Vicodin, Retinol-A…really, how old was Lana to worry about wrinkles already? Ah, the shallowness of those who refused to age.

Not finding anything incriminating, I made a bit of noise returning to the living room. "Something I ate," I said at Lana's questioning look. I glanced at the cookies on the tray. Three of them had one bite gone, then my eyes returned to the plate. I grinned. Cheryl hadn't learned to bake in a day.

Lana waved a hand toward the door. "I'm tired. If you would all excuse me, I'm going to bed." She patted Brock's hand. "Come see me again sometime. You know just how to make a woman feel better. I'd loved to have a friend or two my own age."

Now, I had some questions to ask of my boyfriend. I held the door open for the others, then followed them outside. "Just how did you make her feel better?"

"By listening to her." He smiled.

"You should have seen him." Ruthie opened the car door and climbed in. "He nodded, made little noises in his throat at just the right moment. He kept her talking and comfortable the entire time, but the best thing was he kept her attention off Morgan."

"I can handle myself, sweetheart." Morgan followed her into the car.

"Yeah, but she didn't keep touching your face and hands. You'd best keep an eye on her around Brock, Kelly. She's out to get him."

Brock laughed. "Not a chance. Although I'm not above a little flirting to find out information."

"Did you?" I asked sitting in the front passenger seat.

"Sure did. She's having Rossi over to her house for dinner tomorrow."

"With Cheryl cooking?" My eyebrows rose.

He shrugged. "No idea, but I got us four invited."

"Good job!"

"It's a fancy dinner." His smile widened.

"Ugh." I much preferred jeans and my button-up, chambray shirt.

"You'll have to charm Rossi. He likes them young." Ruthie patted me on the shoulder. "Try acting, and you'll have him nibbling out of your hand, maybe even telling you if he killed Robert."

"I can be charming without acting." I frowned.

"No, you can't. But at least you clean up good."

Brock laughed and started the car. "You'd have him nibbling out of your hand even if you wore sackcloth."

Chapter Seven

Thank goodness Ruthie's closet held a wide variety of gowns. Unless I needed one for a premier or award ceremony—which I could rent, by the way—I didn't spend the money. I'd rather use my funds to build up a nice nest egg or purchase photography equipment.

I smoothed my hand down the knee-length gown with a flounce of lace that flirted around my knees. The black complemented my pale skin and blond hair. A touch of makeup, diamond earrings dangling from my earlobes, and a simple teardrop diamond at my throat, and I was as good as I was going to be.

I wanted to plead sickness. Flirting didn't come easy to me. I'd tried once with Louie the time I'd suspected him of murder, and the director had seen right through my ruse, turning me down flat. Hadn't bolstered my ego the slightest. Now, I'd be trying the same act with a ruthless mob leader. What an idiot I was to allow myself to get lassoed into these things.

"See? You clean up nice." Ruthie, lovely in a gown the color of a dark red wine, entered my room. "You take after me."

I laughed. "I'm a blond, you're a brunette who dyes her hair Lucille Ball red or Elizabeth Taylor black. I have blue eyes, yours are brown. How do we look alike?"

"It's the image, darling." She smiled and handed me a red, beaded clutch that weighed more than it should have. She'd stowed my Ruger inside, sneaky thing. "A touch of color. Come on. The men are waiting."

"I can't believe Lana is hosting a dinner party with her bruises." I followed Ruthie to the living room, my face flushed at the appreciative look in Brock's eyes.

"We've already seen them, so she has nothing to lose."

True. Brock led me to his Mercedes. No vintage car tonight. Ruthie insisted on riding to Lana's in luxury. She wanted to impress Rossi however she could. Schmooze enough and we'd get information, at least that was her train of thought. I didn't think it would be that easy. Not if the information Lisa had dug up on the man was close to being true.

By the time we pulled up to Lana's, I'd managed to worry myself into a full-blown anxiety attack. I breathed like a woman in labor.

Brock pulled me into his arms, telling the others to wait outside the car for us. "We aren't confronting the man about your father, Kelly. We're here to find out who killed Robert."

I nodded. "I know, but the hope is always there."

"If he is the one responsible for your father, what will you do…shoot him?"

I giggled. "I might. Ruthie packed my gun."

He tilted my face to his and laid a gentle kiss on my lips so as not to smear my lipstick. "We're just having dinner, you'll do a bit of flirting, and we'll see what we see. I'm right here beside you."

"It isn't like me to be this anxious." I'd dodged bullets, faced killers, discovered an inner bravery, yet I really felt deep inside me that we were getting closer to whoever killed my father. "Thank you. You always know how to make me feel better."

"So Lana says." He chuckled and pushed the door open. "Stay there and let me be a gentleman for once, please," he said as I started to open my door.

I released the handle and let him treat me like a lady. Slipping my arm in his, we joined the others on the porch. I took a deep breath and reached for the doorbell as the door swung open.

"Come on in. We've had tonight's dinner catered by Staletti's," she whispered. "Cheryl was given the night off."

"Thank goodness," Morgan muttered.

She laughed, her face lighting up enough to make her almost pretty. "Only the best for my childhood friend." She waved us in.

Lana stood with a wide-chested man near the large glass wall that overlooked her pool area. He was a few inches shorter than Brock's six-foot-two. Thick grey hair brushed back from a square face. Bushy eyebrows resembling fuzzy caterpillars hung low over dark eyes. He looked every bit the crime lord.

I forced a smile as Lana introduced us.

"I've been watching your show," Rossi said, kissing the back of Ruthie's hand, then reaching for mine. "Wonderful entertainment, if a bit unrealistic."

"That's show biz." Ruthie grinned. "Realism is boring."

Not for me. It took every bit of willpower not to pull my hand away from his full lips. "It's always nice to meet a fan."

He kept hold of my hand and led me to the table. "Come, gorgeous. Sit by me. Mr. Hanson can sit on your other side to keep me in line." He tossed Brock a wink.

Brock's eyes flashed, but he kept his killer smile on his face. At least he would sit next to me. As long as I had his support, I could bear anything.

"You're more beautiful in person than on the big screen," Rossi said. "I didn't think that was possible." He leaned close. "What perfume are you wearing? It suits you."

My skin crawled. "Inis." I tilted my head, exposing more of my neck.

From under my lashes, I peered up at Brock. Splotches of red rose up his neck.

From the end of the table, Lana's eyes narrowed. She might not like the man, but she also didn't seem to appreciate his attention focused elsewhere. I reached for my water glass and lifted it to my lips. How could I keep the man from getting too close, yet have him let down his guard enough to loosen his tongue?

"What brings you to Beverly Hills, Mr. Rossi?" Ruthie asked, tossing me an apologetic glance.

"Business." He shot Lana a sharp look.

Covert glances shot around the room, and few of them were friendly. Mildred's own cold gaze as she set platters full of Italian food in front of us should have turned Rossi into a block of ice.

"Well done, Mildred. My favorite." Rossi picked up his fork, and for the next fifteen minutes, focused his attention on his food. The man's lack of table manners, smacking of his lips, talking with his mouth full, almost made me lose my appetite.

But, food was one thing we had in common. I did like to eat. Lana focused on her wine, lifting her glass for a refill. Thankfully, Ruthie only sipped hers.

"So, what do you do, Mr. Morgan?" Rossi wiped his mouth with a napkin and waved for a refill of his whiskey.

"I'm Ruthie's fiancé and bodyguard." He crossed his muscled arms, his unblinking gaze focused on Rossi.

"Hmmm." Rossi held his glass to the light and examined the amber liquid inside. "I keep my hired hands out of sight. Employees are to be seen and not heard, much like children."

"He said he's my fiancé," Ruthie added. "No need to hide such a fine man away." She giggled as if she'd had more than half a glass of wine to drink.

Rossi glanced at me. "You two serious?"

"Me and Kelly?" Brock shook his head. "No, we're close, but it's more for publicity." He squeezed my knee under the table. "Neither one of us is ready to settle down right now."

"That's right." I pulled his finger back, trying to peel his hand off me, not being gentle about it. "It wouldn't do for Brock's hottest-man-in-Hollywood status to put a ring on any woman's finger."

Brock hissed as I got too forceful, but his smile never wavered. "Having Kelly on my arm keeps the groupies away."

"Wonderful." Rossi's eyes glittered. "I'd like to invite the four of you, and Lana, of course, to stay in my suite at the New York-New York in Vegas."

"We'd love to," I said, letting go of Brock's hand, "but we still have at least a week of filming on our show."

"A raincheck, then. All you need to do is call the hotel and tell them I invited you." He leaned back in his chair. "I stay at the Mirage most of the time, so my suite will be available when you need it. I'd love to show you around the city." A smile teased at his lips. "Perhaps you'd escort me to dinner one night."

A chill ran down my back at the lecherous glint in his eyes. "I'd be honored."

"Good." He patted my hand. "I knew Kevin Canyon's daughter had to be as smart as he was." His smile widened. "Don't look so shocked. Of course, I knew your father. He was like a tick on my rear end at times, but a good man."

I jerked away from him. "Somebody murdered

him."

"So I heard."

I excused myself and hurried to the restroom. We'd learned nothing more than that Rossi knew my father and couldn't keep dirty thoughts out of his head.

I leaned my hands on the marble vanity top. We'd have to go to Vegas and stay in his suite. I'd have to go to dinner with him…alone. I shuddered. The game would continue until I knew one way or the other whether he had been behind the murder.

My clutch buzzed, and I pulled out my cell phone to see a text from Sarah.

Need help. In jail. Arrested for the murder of Robert.

It looked as if our first course of business would be to free Sarah, then clear her name. Vegas could wait.

Chapter Eight

"Where did you guys just come from?" Lori scowled.

"Dinner party at Lana Doyle's." I set my clutch on her desk with a loud thud.

Her eyes widened. "Do you have a gun in your purse?"

"Uh, yes…Martin Rossi was also a guest. I thought I might need to be prepared."

"Sit down, Kelly. We'll discuss Sarah in a minute. Where are your partners in crime?" She crossed her arms.

"Waiting in the lobby." I retrieved my clutch and set it in my lap out of her reach. I wouldn't put it past her to confiscate my weapon. "I have a permit."

"I'm sure you do. Why in the world would you get involved with someone like Rossi?"

"Because Lana has been seen in his company. If

she killed her husband—"

"All signs point to Sarah."

"What signs?"

"Cyanide poisoning is what killed Robert Doyles. We found a bag of smashed apricots in Ruthie's freezer. No pits."

"So?" I frowned. "I saw apricots and a mortar and pestle on Lana's counter. If that's all the evidence you have, then you might as well arrest Cheryl and every other chef in the city."

She groaned. "The suspect list grows longer each time I talk to you. You do not want to get involved with Rossi."

So everyone kept telling me. I agreed, but then we went in a circle again about not following every lead I came across to find out who killed my father. "You want to find Dad's killer as much as I do. Rossi knew him."

Ah. News to her. "That's not good. He's a known cop killer. Doesn't mean he did the crime, but it does put him at the top of the list. First, we need to solve Doyles' murder. Your father's cold case is on our down time. My down time. Why do I keep including you?"

Because I saw things she didn't. A photographer had a special way of seeing things. "Does Rossi know you or Jason?"

She shrugged. "I don't think so, but it's a possibility. Most men in his profession keep up on law enforcement."

"If we find out he doesn't know you, then the two of you should come with us when we go to Vegas." I'd feel a lot safer with two cops at my side.

"I'll see what's on our books when you go. Chances are, I'll be needed here. You know I'm always trying to solve your father's case. I won't give up."

I reached across the desk and took her hand. "I know." Neither would I.

She sighed. "Let's go release Sarah. With a new suspect, we don't have enough to keep her in."

"Good. Sarah isn't the guilty person."

"We'll see. She has as much motive and means as anyone." She led me from her office.

"Please release my chef." Ruthie glared as we approached.

"I am." Lori exhaled heavily. "She's still a suspect. What does she need all those apricots for?"

"I asked her to make me an apricot cordial." Ruthie's brow furrowed. "Why?"

"Robert was poisoned with cyanide," I explained. "Which is found in apricot pits."

"Well, that will be like the proverbial needle in a haystack. The grocery store is full of apricots."

Lori rolled her eyes. "It isn't full of suspects who wanted Robert dead."

"How do you know?" Ruthie raised her eyebrows. "Maybe he annoyed one of the baggers too many times."

"Lord, help me." Lori told us to wait while she got Sarah from the holding cell. She returned a few minutes later with a flannel-gowned, fuzzy-robed, bunny slipper-wearing Sarah.

"You took her in her pajamas?" Ruthie sighed. "The humility."

"We don't usually ask someone to dress when we arrest them." Lori unlocked the handcuffs. "Don't leave town."

"As if I have anywhere to go." Head high, she shuffled from the police station, leaving the rest of us to follow.

"What about Vegas?" Ruthie's eyes widened. "Surely, she can go with us."

Lori shook her head. "No, she cannot. Do not push me on this."

Ruthie tossed her head and stormed after our chef. Friends one minute, enemies the next, whether it regarded Sarah or Lori.

With a resigned glance at the men, I followed the women to Brock's car where I squeezed into the backseat with the other two women, leaving the front for Morgan. Sarah sat between us, arms crossed, back hunched, face scowling.

"I should have remained homeless," she said. "It's been nothing but trouble since getting a job and a roof over my head."

"Don't be ungrateful. We'll get to the bottom of all this." Ruthie glanced sideways. "You saved my Kelly's life, and now we'll save yours."

"You think someone wants to kill me?" Sarah glanced from Ruthie to me.

"No, she means we'll help clear your name." I glared at my grandmother. "She doesn't always use the best choice of words."

The next morning, I laced up my running shoes, clipped the leash on Shutterbug's collar, and took a much overdue jog. Guilt riddled through me at how

I'd been neglecting my poor furry girl recently. Louie didn't like dogs on the set anymore since I'd given Sassy to my grandmother as a gift. The noisy little dog grated on his nerves. So no Sassy, no Shutterbug, and no Brutus.

We trotted at a leisurely pace down the sidewalk to limber up. I held my dog back until we reached a track through a park, then we'd run all out. I couldn't wait to burn off some frustrations and mull over reasons, other than gambling, that someone would want Robert dead.

He had a gambling problem. Was dead broke. An adulterer. Three things that pointed to his widow as the guilty person. Next in line was Cheryl. Maybe Robert tried to break things off with her. Having two women on a leash would be expensive, right?

Why would Rossi want him dead? He couldn't pay back his debt from the grave. Rossi couldn't have known that Lana would make an "agreement" with him if Robert was gone. I pretty much discounted Sarah. She had a good thing going as our chef. Why mess that up? My bet was on Lana or Cheryl.

The soles of my shoes slapped the pavement as we veered right down a street toward an expanse of green next to a small pond. Shutterbug let out a happy yip as we increased our speed. I smiled and nodded at other walkers and joggers as we passed, circling the pond for another go-around.

Loud voices caused me to slow down and tighten my grip on the leash. My German shepherd didn't take kindly to fights and wouldn't hesitate to put herself between the participants. Otherwise, she was as gentle as a lamb unless I was threatened. Then, watch out, whoever got between us.

Shutterbug growled low in her throat. Her hair bristled.

"Shh." I pulled her behind a bush and parted the branches.

Two men I didn't recognize stood nose-to-nose. Red faces and clenched fists could mean they were seconds away from throwing punches.

"I'm not going to rough up a woman," the young blond one said.

"You'll do what you're paid to do." The older one, dark hair with beard stubble, gave the other man a shove. "That nosy actress can't get involved. She needs a warning."

My heart stopped. They weren't talking about me, were they?

"The old woman is no threat to us."

Ruthie!

"No, but her granddaughter is."

They were talking about me. I moved slowly backward and raced for my car. I needed to let Lori know I was once again in danger. And I hadn't even done anything yet. Obviously, Rossi hadn't bought my flirtation act, unless finding out who my father was cleared things up for him. Either way, those men wanted to put a beat down on me and Ruthie.

Once in the car, I locked the doors and called Lori as I sped toward home. "I'm in trouble."

"What's new?" She sighed.

I explained about the conversation at the park. "Can you meet me at home?"

"Ten minutes." Click.

Ruthie wasn't home. I sprinted from room to room calling her name until Sarah stepped out of the kitchen.

"What in the world are you doing?" She held a wooden spoon smeared with red sauce.

"Where's my grandmother?"

"I sent her to get sugar for the cordial." She paled. "What's wrong?"

"I overheard two men saying they needed to give both Ruthie and me a warning." I plopped onto the sofa and patted the cushion next to me. Shutterbug obliged and laid her head in my lap. When the doorbell rang, she sprang off the furniture and barked until she reached the door. Her barks turned to whines. Good. Not someone intent on harming me.

I opened the door and let Lori and Jason in. "We need to find Ruthie."

"Where is she?" Jason already headed for the car.

"To get sugar."

His shoulders sagged. "That could be anywhere. Did you try calling her?" He pulled his cellphone from his pocket.

"No, she never has her phone with—"

"Ruthie? Where are you?" Jason continued his way to the car leaving me feeling stupid. "Stay inside. I'll be there to get you. I'll explain on the way back."

"Why don't we have Sarah make us some coffee and you explain to me what exactly you heard." Lori shooed me back to the sofa.

"Coffee coming right up." Sarah rushed back to the kitchen.

I repeated everything I'd told Lori while driving home. "Where's Morgan? Why isn't he with Ruthie?"

"Morgan had a checkup. He can't be with her every minute of the day. I thought she never drove anywhere."

"She took an Uber," Sarah yelled from the kitchen.

"We don't know that the men were talking about you."

I scowled. "What other grandmother/granddaughter actors do you know? Of course they were talking about us. It's too coincidental otherwise."

"Just trying to keep you from freaking out."

"I'm not freaking out." Well, maybe a little. My nerves were strung as tight as Ruthie's pantyhose.

Sarah set the coffee tray on the table. "Why don't you try calling her? Hearing her voice might make you feel better."

"What a great idea." I pulled my phone from the thin belt around my waist with its hidden pocket and dialed Ruthie's voice.

"Hello?"

"Are you okay?"

"Of course, I am. Jason picked me up from the store. Wasn't that nice of him? Why do you ask?"

"He hasn't told you anything?" I shook my head at Lori and put the phone on speaker mode.

"Told me what? Turn here, Jason."

"Someone's following us pretty close," he said.

"I'm going to try and lose them."

"Just let them pass," Ruthie told him. "Well, that was rude."

"What?" My gaze clashed with Lori's.

"They bumped us from the back. Watch out!"

A screech of metal.

Ruthie screamed.

Silence.

Chapter Nine

"Let's go." Lori darted out the door, staring at her cell phone.

"Where?" Tears streamed down my face as I grabbed the end of Shutterbug's leash. I couldn't lose Ruthie this way. She was the only family I have left, besides my newly-found brother.

"I put a tracker on both your phones months ago." She jumped into the passenger seat of my car. "Drive. I'll give you directions. Head to Santa Monica Boulevard." Her gaze locked on her phone screen.

We found Jason's vehicle twisted around a palm tree three miles down the boulevard. A group of bystanders stared at the wreckage. We found no sign of my grandmother or brother, other than what looked like a lot of blood to me, but a piece of paper flapped from the twisted windshield wiper.

"Where did they go?" Lori whirled to face an

elderly man walking a poodle, then handed the paper to me.

"I saw a man and a woman run that way." He pointed up the street.

"This is the only warning you'll get," I read aloud before unclipping Shutterbug's leash and shoving the note in my pocket. "Find Ruthie." Why run if the warning came too late? The good thing…they couldn't run if they were seriously injured.

The dog took off in the direction the man pointed, her nose to the ground. I raced after her, Lori on my heels. The detective called Morgan and told him where to meet us.

We followed Shutterbug a few blocks and in between two houses before coming to a stop outside an iron gate. "There's no way Ruthie could climb this." I stared at a foot of fence above my head.

"Because I didn't." The lid of a large plastic trash bin next to me lifted and Ruthie peered over the edge. Blood poured from a gash under her bangs. Jason, looking just as beat up, climbed out of the recycling bin, then helped Ruthie out.

"The two of you should be in the hospital." I put my arm around Ruthie's waist and let her lean on me. "Why'd you run from the car?"

"We thought we were being chased. A man seemed overly interested in us after the accident." Jason wiped something gooey off his hands and onto his pants. "This is as far as Ruthie could go. I think she has a concussion."

"Of course, someone was interested," Lori said. "You were in an accident. Ugh."

Morgan thundered toward us. He took one look at Ruthie, scooped her into his arms, and hurried to his waiting truck. "See you guys at the hospital. Jason?"

"I'll ride with you. I'm not feeling very well."

"It might be the piece of metal sticking out of your side," Lori said. "Kelly and I will drop the dog off at her place and meet you at the hospital."

I called Brock on our way home. He met us at the hospital half an hour later. "How is she?" he asked.

"No idea. She looked pretty shaken up when we found her, a bit bloody and bruised," I said, "but they had run a few blocks before hiding, so I don't think she's in mortal danger."

Lori used her clout as law enforcement to get us into the hospital room where Jason and Ruthie, separated by a curtain pulled half way shut, waited. My grandmother wore a startling white bandage around her head and an upset expression.

"I don't know why they couldn't just slap on a Band-Aid. This thing—" she whirled her finger around her head, "is messing up my hair."

I choked back a nervous laugh and gave her a hug. "How are you feeling otherwise?"

"Just grand. They gave me a pain med. Jason has to have surgery."

He leaned forward, waved and gave us a dopey grin. "The doctor wasn't impressed that I carried a piece of the car around with me while we ran."

Two orderlies entered the room. "Time to go, Officer Banks," one of them said. "He'll be moved into a different room after recovery. The doctor will be in to talk to you about Ms. Canyon in a few minutes."

I gripped Jason's hand as he passed. "I'll be here when you get out of surgery."

"Okeydoke." He grinned and waved again as they wheeled him away.

"That poor boy is as high as a kite," Ruthie said. "Some people just can't handle their medication."

I met Brock's amused glance as a woman in a white coat entered the room. Her name tag identified her as Doctor Reynolds. She paused at the sight of Brock, her mouth dropping open, then her lips tightened together. Seems professionalism won over fan adoration. "Ms. Canyon is suffering from a concussion. We'd like to keep her overnight."

"Nope." Ruthie shook her head, then grimaced at the movement.

"I'll stay right here with you, sweetheart." Morgan patted her hand. "If the doctor says you're staying, then you will stay."

"They won't let me have wine, Mark."

"No alcohol while taking pain meds," the doctor said. "You'll be just fine in a couple of days. Officer Banks will need to stay at least one day longer, more if the metal damaged anything internally, although I don't think so. Any of you family?"

"I'm his partner," Lori said, "and this is his sister."

"Only you two will be allowed to see him tonight." Doctor Reynolds glanced from under lowered lashes at Brock. "Sorry."

"No apology necessary. I'll be comfortable

enough in the waiting room." Brock smiled.

"You might want to use the smaller one at the end of the hall. The other is a bit crowded." She returned his smile and left us to listen to Ruthie's bickering.

An hour later, Doctor Reynolds led Lori and me to Jason's room and Brock to the more private waiting room. Hollywood always had an alternate place for celebrities to hide in these types of situations. I was torn between waiting for Jason and staying with Ruthie. The more serious injury won out. That, and the fact Lori and I could discuss what had happened without my grandmother's interruption.

"There's a few things I don't understand." I smoothed the note on the bed Jason would later occupy. "Why run them off the road, hang around while they ran off and risk exposure? Why leave a note that can be traced for fingerprints and handwriting?"

"Stupid hired hands?" Lori flopped into the salmon-colored vinyl chair. "Wouldn't be the first time we've run across fools who'd do anything to make a quick dollar. If I'm right, then they'd want to see the result, right?"

True. I'd had a run-in with a Spiderman impersonator and a gang member during an initiation. This wasn't a far stretch by any means.

"I saw them," Jason mumbled as an orderly wheeled him into the room. He groaned as they transferred him to the bed.

I grabbed the note from the blanket before he could lie on it. "Are you coherent enough to talk to us?" I glanced from him to Lori. "Should we wait until later?"

"Let's see what he can tell us. I don't want too much time to pass without following up on any leads."

Jason nestled into a comfortable position, flashing a pretty nurse a smile as she raised the head of the bed and put a pillow behind him. "I got a good sight of the truck, too. Forest green, Ford 150, early model. Two Hispanic men, early twenties. Couldn't see well enough to pick out any tattoo symbols, although it seems they had them."

"Wow, bro, you got a lot from the short amount of time you had." Impressive. Especially since Ruthie had to have been screaming in his ear.

"Ruthie leaned over the back seat and watched them most of the time. I was kind of busy driving."

Ooops. Wrong on my part. Still, knowing she kept her cool had me impressed.

Lori balanced her elbows on her knees and leaned closer to the bed. "You said the two men watched you run off. Where's the truck?"

His eyes widened. "Didn't you see it? It was parked in the driveway of the house we crashed in front of."

With a glance at me, Lori darted from the room, me on her heels. "See you later," I called over my shoulder.

"The truck won't still be there," I told Lori, sliding into the driver's seat of my car.

"There might be tire tracks, or someone could have gotten the license plate, or the owners of the house might be home." She continued to rattle off reasons for us to speed back to the scene of the crime.

"If you're going to keep riding in my vehicle," I said, "you need to put a light and siren in the glove compartment or trunk."

"Not a chance. You'd take advantage of it."

"No, I wouldn't." I grinned. "But Ruthie would every time she needed to get her hair done."

"Where's the note?"

I drove with one hand and pulled it out of my pocket. "It's a bit crumbled and has my fingerprints all over it. Sorry."

"We might still get something off it." Lori dropped it into a paper sack. I kept a few bags in my car for moments such as this. I was a policeman's daughter, after all.

"The two guys I overheard in the park weren't Hispanic, nor did they have tattoos." I drummed my fingers on the steering wheel. "Middlemen?"

Lori shrugged. "Maybe. I'll need you to speak with a sketch artist. Jason will do the same once he's had some rest. We'll connect the dots eventually."

I turned onto Santa Monica Boulevard as a truck matching the description of the one my brother gave us turned off. I whipped the wheel around and sped after them.

"A little warning next time." Lori rubbed her head. "Glass and my temple aren't friends."

"Sorry. I wasn't expecting them to be here. Why'd they hang around?"

"No idea. Catch up with them."

"I'll follow, but I will not engage. I do not want

anything to happen to this car. She's irreplaceable."

"If you lose them, I'll arrest you for obstruction of justice."

"Threats do not work with me." Liar. I pressed harder on the accelerator.

Chapter Ten

Since the aqua paint job on the Camaro didn't exactly let us blend in with the other vehicles on the road, it didn't take those in the truck long to know they were being followed. "How far do we want to go?"

"As far as it takes for me to worry about our safety," Lori said. "When did you become such a scaredy-cat?"

"It started the first time someone tried to kill me and escalated the second time. I have no desire to repeat the experience." Although I had written a book each time, both of which became best-sellers. I could write one about this mystery too, and fill in the blanks. That's how experienced I felt at staring down the barrel of a gun.

The truck turned off the interstate. "I am not going to East L.A." I whipped the wheel down the frontage road and headed back toward the hospital.

"Turn around. Ugh. You've lost them." Lori pounded the dashboard.

"I'm a civilian. I'm not going into gangsterville." I set my jaw and continued in the same direction.

Lori sighed. "You're right. I shouldn't have asked you to. Can we at least return to the accident site?"

"Yes." I switched directions, not stopping until we pulled up a few feet in front of the house where Jason had crashed. The car had been removed, but tiny slivers of glass still glittered from the pavement. Not enough to puncture a tire, but enough to say what had happened there.

The spectators were gone. No car sat in the driveway of the house to our right. "Now what?"

Lori shoved open her door. "We go knocking on doors." She cut me a sharp look. "Why don't you get your license or join the police academy so you can be more than a civilian informant?"

"No, thanks. I prefer doing what I want when I want."

"And skirting the law a lot of times."

I grinned. "Only because you allow it, since we have a common goal."

"The new chief can't find out you're helping." She headed toward the front door of the house.

"Why?" I hurried to catch up. "Do you think he's dirty, too?"

"I'm not discounting anyone at this point. I've made that mistake before."

I nodded. Her former partner, Sawyer, had been as bad as they come. So had Detective Warren, her partner after that. I couldn't blame her for thinking Chief Foster might follow the same path. My father had known something about the dirty cops on the force and died for his trouble.

"Wait a minute." I studied the mansion in front of us. I'd been here before. "This is where the former actress, Iris Beacon, lives. She'll talk to us if she's home." I rang the bell. Winchester chimes sang a pretty tune. A few months ago, Ruthie and I visited under circumstances similar to the one we were here about again.

A few minutes later, Iris opened the door just enough to peer out. "Kelly?"

"May we come in?"

She stepped back. "Of course. Are those horrible young men gone?"

I nodded. "This is Detective Lawrence. Did you see what happened?"

"Of course, I did. I don't miss a thing, sweetie. Sit down. I'll put on some tea." She strolled away, a silk caftan billowing behind her.

I sat next to Lori on a damask sofa about as soft as a rock and shifted, trying to find a comfortable position. "Iris is the neighborhood gossip. Knows everything there is to know about everyone. Strange, considering she rarely leaves her home anymore."

"It's most likely because of all the cameras." Lori pointed to one in a corner, another by the front door. "I bet she has a console of monitors set up somewhere. This woman could be a gold mine."

"Yes, to everything you just said." Iris set a china tea set on a carved, wooden coffee table. "A woman living alone can't be too careful."

"No ma'am, you can't." Lori smiled and pulled a notepad from her inside jacket pocket. "What did you see?"

"Have some tea first, dear. Then I'll show you. Much better than trying to remember all the details." Iris sat across from us. "As soon as it happened, I pulled out my cell phone and saved the recording." She tapped a well-manicured finger against her temple. "I'm a smart one."

So smart that the tea, which she'd produced awfully fast in my opinion, tasted more like a chardonnay than an Earl's Grey. Exactly the type of refreshment Ruthie would enjoy. As for me, I set the cup back on the tray next to Lori's.

Iris took a sip. "Ooops." She took the tray back to the kitchen and returned with a pitcher of water and three glasses. "Sorry."

Lori's wide-eyed expression didn't look favorable as to how much of Iris's information she'd believe. Iris smiled. "I was quite happy to see that Ruthie could still run for a woman of her age. Of course, the young man practically dragged her, but I would have had to lie down and die."

"Die? Did you believe them to be in immediate danger?" Lori tilted her head. "Other than being run off the road, that is."

"The men did have guns." Iris poured us each a glass of water. "I like to piddle around in my flowers. Helps keep me apprised of what goes on in the neighborhood. Earlier today, I heard metal hit metal and climbed on a crate to look over the fence…"

I bet she kept a crate there for that reason. I hid my smile behind my glass.

"That's when I saw the truck hit the back of the squad car. Stupid really. Don't they realize they'll go to jail for ramming a police car?" She shook her head. "Then, the young man helped Ruthie out of the car. The men in the truck got out. Weird thing was they all stared at each other for a minute, then Ruthie and her young man started running."

"May we see the tape now?" Lori stood.

"Of course." Iris led us to a room off the kitchen. "State of the art." She turned on the light to reveal three monitors. One filmed the inside of the house, one the back yard and one the front.

Lori lowered herself into the chair in front of the one aimed at the front of the house and pressed a button, stopping when the film showed the vehicles approaching. She peered closer at the screen.

I watched over her shoulder as the truck rammed the back of the squad car, sending it into a palm tree. The occupants of both cars exited, just as Iris had said. Jason said something, then one of the men raised his gun. "It looks like he told them to run."

"You're right. This was strictly to warn them," Lori said. "No shots fired, and they were given the opportunity to get away. I can't make out what Jason said, though."

"He asked them what they wanted." Iris studied her manicure. "That's it, then they were told to run. It seemed like something out of a movie. This city is never boring, is it?"

"Not for a minute." I straightened. "Can you get

facial recognition on those two men?"

"I'm going to try." Lori popped the disc from the computer. "You've been a big help, Ms. Beacon." She handed Iris a business card. "Please contact me if you remember anything else."

"I most certainly will. You two come visit me anytime." She walked us out, pointing out not a crate, but a large footstool for her to use to spy on her neighbors.

Leaving there, we headed back to the hospital to speak with Jason and Ruthie again. Brock no longer sat in the waiting room, but in Ruthie's room. Guilt ripped through me. I'd forgotten all about him when Lori and I took off so fast.

"That's all right," he said when I explained. "Sometimes you don't have time to look someone up. I might have been in the cafeteria getting coffee or in the restroom, which would have slowed you down."

I wrapped my arms around him. "You are one of a kind."

He kissed the top of my head. "I actually fell asleep and only realized you were gone a few minutes ago. Morgan came looking for me to tell me Ruthie was awake. That's when I knew you were gone. It really isn't a problem."

I didn't deserve him. I glanced to where Ruthie and Morgan whispered. "What are the two of you up to?"

"Nothing." Ruthie couldn't look more guilty if she tried.

"Liar."

"Fine. Morgan is going out looking for these

two scoundrels, and I want to go with him."

"Absolutely not," we said in unison.

She crossed her arms and glared. "I'm an adult and can make my own decisions."

Opting on the side of agreeing with her, I said, "Of course, but you shouldn't make any major decisions while on pain medication. Let's discuss this tomorrow when you're home."

Still peeved, she agreed. "Where did you and Lori rush off to?"

I explained about the chase and interview with Iris. Not the smartest thing because it got her riled up again.

"You're having fun without me." She flounced onto her side, putting her back to us.

I chose to attribute her sullen attitude to pain and medication. "I'm going to check on Jason."

"Me, too," Lori and Brock said.

I mouthed, "sorry" to Morgan. He's the one marrying her. He might as well get used to how the rest of his life would be.

Jason's eyes popped open the minute we stepped into his room. "What did you find out?"

Lori recounted the afternoon's events. "Anything we missed?"

"No." He sighed. "I didn't stay to ask questions when they told us to run. I expected a bullet in the back at any minute. Glad it didn't happen."

"Me, too." I sat next to the bed and took his hand. "I'd hate to lose a brother I recently discovered I have. How's the side?"

"Sore, but nothing vital was damaged." He grimaced and lifted the bed to a sitting position.

"I'll be out of commission for a day or two though, so if you don't mind, I'll move in with you and Ruthie and play bodyguard."

"I don't mind at all. In fact, I insist." Morgan would want to accompany us to the set every day and could now be free at night to do his sleuthing. He wasn't one to sit back when the woman he loved was in danger. Neither was Brock, actually. I glanced at his stony expression.

"I'm moving in."

"Knew that was coming," Lori said. "The more around, the safer it is. You'll get no arguments from me."

"Sorry to leave you partner-less again." Jason frowned.

"I'd rather have it that way. You're the only one on the force I trust at this point." Her phone dinged, and she glanced at the screen. "Speaking of the devil, Chief Foster wants my report on his desk in an hour. Great. He'll want to know what I've been doing all day."

"Tell him you've been with me." Jason grinned. "I'll back up your story. No need for him to know you've been gallivanting with my trouble-making sister."

"Good idea. He won't like to know that." She slipped her phone back into its holder. "I'll come later this evening to check on you."

"Be careful." Jason grew serious. "The bad guys know you were in the car chasing them. Until we figure out who put them up to this, none of us are safe."

Chapter Eleven

After picking Ruthie up from the hospital the next morning, I sat on the patio, notepad in my lap, and tried to make sense of all that had gone on. What a mess! Some sleuth I was. I had no clue as to how to proceed. I hoped to get a clue while the others fussed over Ruthie in the house.

I idly scratched Shutterbug's ears and watched as Brutus and Sassy frolicked across the lawn. I smiled at the antics of a mastiff and a Yorkie.

"What's on your mind?" Brock dropped into the lounge chair next to me and stretched out his long legs.

"Trying to figure out who killed Robert Doyles."

He nodded toward the empty notepad. "Looks like you've got a good start." He gave me a crooked smile, then leaned over and kissed me. "I've a little time before I have to be on set. Shoot."

"Bad choice of words, Mr. Handsome."

He laughed. "All right, Cutie Canyon."

I tilted my head and frowned. "That's the nickname you picked for me?"

"Yep." He looked quite pleased with himself as he folded his arms behind his head. "You're the cutest thing I've ever seen."

I rolled my eyes, but couldn't stop a smile from forming. "Okay. Concentrate. Doyles faked drowning, then acted sick during the ceremony, something that ended up being true. He didn't die instantly, although he'd been poisoned by cyanide. Slow portions over time?" I chewed the end of my pen. "If so, it had to be someone close to him, like his wife or mistress, right?"

"Or the housekeeper. Apricot pits aren't hard to get a hold of. Neither is cyanide."

"Then the two thugs who ran Jason and Ruthie off the road. That looks like a dead end." Unless someone headed to East L.A., which I didn't want to do. "We could just go on with our lives as usual and wait for someone to come to us. They always do, thinking we know more than we do."

"I can't decide if that's a blessing or a curse." He took my hand. "You've brought justice to several deaths, so we might be able to call what you have a gift."

"That's stretching it." I laughed and wrote down the names of the three women who lived in the Doyles' household. Other people? Sarah? No. She didn't kill her ex-husband. And what if she saw my notes? I might lose a special friend.

I tapped the pen on the paper. All three names

had the same motive. Robert Doyles was a cheater. Oh. I added Martin Rossi's name. Doyles owed him a lot of money. That was a motive. Good. I was getting somewhere.

Brock leaned over to kiss me again, then stood. "I can see you're lost in the world of mystery. I'll see you after work. How long has Louie given you and Ruthie off?"

"Until Monday." Three days, the inconsiderate oaf. Lisa's makeup talent would be put to the test covering up the wound on Ruthie's head.

I climbed out of my chair and walked Brock to his car, Shutterbug on my heels. "I'll see you at dinner."

"I'll be back with an overnight bag. Might as well move in with everyone else." A quick kiss to my forehead and he got in his Mercedes and left.

As I turned to go back in the house, Shutterbug's intense stare at something across the street got my attention. A low rumble started in her throat. I turned.

The tallest of the two men I'd seen conversing in the park smoked a cigarette, his gaze locked on mine. He put his fingers into the shape of a gun and pointed it in my direction. His hand moved toward his pocket and he stepped off the curb toward me.

I uttered the German word for attack, "*Angriff.*" Shutterbug darted toward the man with me as close on her heels as my two legs could follow her four.

The man yelped, dropped his cigarette, and thundered down the sidewalk. He darted behind a recycling can left out by a neighbor and grabbed the lowest branch of a mesquite tree. Not exactly the strongest variety and promptly landed on his back on the concrete.

Trying to catch my breath, I stood over him while Shutterbug bared her teeth. "Why are you watching me? Are you responsible for my grandmother's accident?"

"Call off your dog."

"Not a chance. Answer me or I'll give the command for her to bury her teeth in your throat." I narrowed my eyes.

Morgan must have seen our chase through the front window because he joined us and hauled the man to his feet. He whirled him around and cuffed him, then slammed him against a cinder-block fence. "Talk."

"I can't tell you who I work for or that person will kill me."

Smart not giving away whether he worked for a man or a woman. "Why me and my family?" I planted my fists on my hips.

"Because you're nosy?" He shrugged. "I just do as I'm told. You don't want to mess with these people, lady."

"So I've heard." I pulled out my cell phone and called Lori who said she'd be there in fifteen minutes to collect our suspect. "I know you're behind running Ruthie off the road. I ought to kill you myself." I kicked his shin for good measure.

"That's assault!"

"Sue me." I commanded Shutterbug to sit and waved at Iris Beacon who peeked over a fence on the other side of the street. Five minutes later, she rushed over to us with a plate of cookies.

"Not for you," she told the stranger. "These are for good people and dogs only." She tossed him a glare and Shutterbug a chocolate-chip cookie. "One cookie won't hurt this sweet little thing. But that's all you get, beautiful girl."

"Thanks." Morgan grabbed three.

I grinned and nabbed one for myself and two for Lori. I loved when people fawned over my fur baby. "Detective Lawrence will enjoy these."

"Oh, good. I've more news for her." She plopped on the sidewalk. "I'll wait." She studied the man against the wall. "You were here yesterday. I saw you in the crowd."

I whipped around to face him. "Making sure the job got done?"

He gave a one-shoulder shrug. "It's no crime to be on public property."

"It is if you purposely crashed into my grandmother and a police officer."

"I was just following orders. I didn't know they couldn't drive." He sneered.

Almost thirty minutes passed before Lori arrived. The only one of us not growing impatient was my dog. Her dark eyes remained riveted on the stranger.

"Sorry." Lori stepped onto the sidewalk. "Fill me in."

I did, then stepped back and let Iris take over.

"Remember my telling you that nothing escapes my eye?" With Morgan's help, she got to her feet. "I might forget, but it comes back to me eventually. This man—" She jabbed a thumb in the stranger's direction. "—was here in the crowd relishing his evil deed." Her hand got too close and she jammed her thumb into his eye. "He could have killed my friend. Lock him up."

"Ow, lady." He blinked. Since he wore handcuffs, he couldn't wipe the tears forming from the contact. "Uh-oh."

I whirled to see Ruthie marching toward us. She'd removed the bandage and managed to style her hair to cover the wound. Unfortunately, no amount of makeup could cover the bruises on her face. She stopped in front of the stranger and slapped him.

"I have no idea why I did that except that you must have had a hand in permanently messing up my hairline."

Morgan didn't bother to hide his grin. A nerve twitched above Lori's right eye. Iris cheered. I broke into laughter. Leave it to my friends and family to make something criminal hilarious.

"I've been assaulted by everyone here except the law enforcement officer," the man said, glaring at Lori. "Aren't you going to do something?"

"Yes, sir. I'm taking you to jail. Tell your sorrows to the judge." She glanced back at me. "I'll be over once I have him squared away."

Except for Iris, who insisted she had to get back to work watching the neighborhood, the rest of us trooped back to the house. "Ruthie, you shouldn't have come outside. You have a concussion," I told her as she settled herself on the couch with Sassy.

"I had to see what was going on. You should have stalled Lori. It took me a long time to get ready, then it was all over. I'll die of boredom sitting here."

"It's one day." I rolled my eyes and headed for the kitchen. "Sarah, we could use some coffee."

She nodded, idly drying the same plate several times. "I've been thinking."

"About?"

"Who might have killed Robert." She cut me a quick glance before setting the very dry plate in the cupboard. "I don't like Lana, but I don't think she killed him. I do think she might have had something to do with his death, indirectly, that is. Have you had your computer girl research her?"

"We focused mainly on Robert, why?"

"Because, Lana grew up in Vegas. Maybe she knew Rossi before Robert's gambling got out of control."

"That's great reasoning." I patted her on the shoulder. "I'll call Lisa right now. Maybe she'll know something before Lori returns this evening."

I called Lisa who agreed to do some deep digging. If she found something, she'd bring it over later rather than risk a phone call. Big Brother had ears everywhere. Since my house had been bugged before, I agreed, then hung up and asked Morgan to sweep the place for listening devices.

"I did that last night. We're clean." He tucked an afghan around Ruthie's legs.

She promptly flung it off. "Too hot."

"You're the most difficult woman to take care of that I've ever met." Morgan glared down at her.

"Taken care of many?" She glowered.

"Good heavens." I snapped my fingers for Shutterbug to follow me outside. The two of them bickering was the last thing I needed. They'd never fought until getting engaged. If putting a ring on someone's finger caused them to act like those two, then I'd stay single, thank you very much. Not that Brock had asked me to marry him, and we were both fairly mild-tempered, but why rush things? If marriage made a person nervous enough to act like someone they weren't, was it worth it?

"Here's your coffee." Sarah handed me a mug, then sat in the empty seat next to me. "Gracious, those two act like children sometimes."

"Only recently. Ruthie is scared out of her mind of getting married. She wasn't married to my grandfather, although they were together until he died. I guess a common-law type of thing isn't as scary to her."

"If she's worried about her money, she can have him sign a prenup. I did with Robert. Of course, that's why I ended up penniless and on the streets."

"He had money when you married?"

"Loads of it. His family owned oil wells in Texas. The gambling started with his grandfather and trickled down. I thought Robert had a grasp on it. Guess I was wrong." She crossed her arms and stared at the pool. "I still can't believe he tried to fake his drowning. That man has never been the sharpest nail in the box. Not to speak ill of the dead."

I wouldn't stop her. The more she talked, the more I got to know the deceased. The more I knew the deceased, the closer I got to catching his killer.

Chapter Twelve

Lori rang the door at seven, Lisa right behind her. I let them in while Sarah rushed to the kitchen to cut a cake she'd baked that afternoon. I glanced around outside for Brock before closing the door. He'd texted me an hour ago that he was running late, but still should have been here by then. My heart lodged in my throat. After Ruthie's accident, I tended to fear the worse.

"He's fine." Lori patted my shoulder on her way past. "Stop worrying."

"He called you?"

"No, Jason mentioned Brock was stopping by to visit him before coming here. I guess the two got involved talking."

"Did you put a tracker on his phone, too?" I closed the door.

"I have one on all of your phones. Forgive the intrusion, but with everyone here always getting into trouble, I made an executive decision." She smiled and dropped into an overstuffed easy chair.

When she put it that way, how could I be upset? I felt safer knowing someone could always find me as long as I had my phone with me.

"Ready to hear what I found out?" Lisa rubbed her hands together. "I should work for the FBI."

"Not a chance," Ruthie said. "You're too good at makeup."

"By all means cement your future on Ruthie's wishes." I laughed and curled up on one corner of the sofa. "Tell us, Lisa."

"Lana Doyles was born Lucy Brown, aka Stiletto. She's Italian and used to dance on a pole at Rossi's little casino in Vegas. That's probably where Robert Doyles met her." She perched on the arm of the sofa. "Here's where it gets good. I told you she was seen around town with Rossi…well, it seems they were actually an item when she danced for him, but he never committed to a relationship because it would hurt his reputation to marry an exotic dancer, or so the rumor goes." She grinned. "Seems he has some misguided morals."

"Why now?" I asked. "Lana is as broke as her husband."

"Oh, my dear friend, that's where you are wrong. I found a rather hefty bank account under the name, Lucy Stiletto. Our pretty little widow has been squirreling her husband's money away for a rainy day."

Lori grinned. "You really should be with the FBI."

"Stop trying to get her to stop doing makeup."

Ruthie reached up to take a plate of cake offered by Sarah. "Why didn't you put money away?"

"Because I believed my wedding vows." Sarah sniffed and turned to offer Morgan a plate. "I signed a prenup believing in the happily-ever-after. Apparently, Lana is smarter than me." She glanced from Morgan to Ruthie. "The two of you, stop your childishness and figure out whether your love is worth moving forward. You're driving us all crazy."

Silence fell upon the room like a bucket of ice water as we waited for Ruthie to explode. Instead, she shrugged and took a bite of her red velvet cake. "This is delicious. My favorite."

A key turned in the lock of the front door. I turned to greet Brock, since he was the only one not already there who had a key.

Jason, staggering under the weight of Brock, who held his arm to his ribcage, entered and slammed the door shut. "Lock it. I think we were followed."

Lori raced for the door and threw the deadbolt. "What happened?"

Jason lowered Brock onto the sofa, then collapsed next to him. I jumped to my feet to give them room. "Brock came to the hospital to pick me up. The doctor said I could come here if I took it easy. I knew you were going to discuss the case and wanted to be here." He took a deep shuddering breath. "Dude, you're heavy."

"Sorry." Brock coughed. "Three goons jumped us as soon as we neared the car. They didn't touch Jason...probably knew he was a cop." He winced.

"…but sure gave me a beating."

Sarah thrust a rag filled with ice into my hand, and I held it gently to his bruised cheek. "You're holding your side."

"Might have a cracked rib, but we didn't think…we should risk going back inside. The three men took off when a man and woman approached. Jason helped me into the car…and here we are."

"I think you need to go back." I cupped his other cheek. "Cracked ribs are nothing to be taken lightly."

"I'm not, believe me… Hurts like the dickens. Just let me rest for a minute."

"I know someone I can call to give them a safe ride back." Morgan stepped onto the back patio to make a call.

"Would you recognize the two men?" Lori asked. "Were they the same ones who ran you off the road?"

Jason shrugged. "These three wore hoodies, but my guess is they were gang members earning extra money. Not hard to do around here."

"But why Brock?" I frowned. "I understand warning me or Ruthie, but him?"

Brock grinned, his lip splitting where a scab had barely started to form. "Because I've been doing some questioning…around the set."

"Do tell." I sat on the floor and peered up at him.

"Your show wasn't the only one Robert was backing, but it's… the only one with funding to still continue…thanks to Ruthie."

"Which increases our suspect list," Lori said.

"We could have disgruntled actors, directors, etc."

Ruthie shook her head. "Celebrities do not kill people. It's bad for their image."

"Remember Doug?" My eyes widened. Ruthie's former manager had been as ruthless as they come. "And Amber Jacobson?"

"Neither were celebrities. A manager and a movie-star wannabe." She waved a dismissive hand. "If you think it's someone involved with filmmaking, you'll have to look to someone behind the scenes. A lot of people are out of work when a film or show ends."

Lori paced the area behind the sofa. "There's hundreds of people."

"That's why I was asking around," Brock said. "I've a list of people who were bad-mouthing Robert. It will take some working through…but your killer might be on here." He pulled a crumbled napkin from his pocket and handed it to Lori.

I snatched it from her hand and darted for the office, slamming the door. I had to make a photocopy or I'd never know who was on the list.

"Kelly Canyon, open this door." Lori did not sound pleased.

I laid the napkin on the copier, pressed the key, and hoped Lori didn't knock the door down while it copied. When it finished, I folded the duplicate and shoved it into my bra. Short of arrest, I wasn't turning it over. I unlocked the door and handed the napkin to Lori. Our gazes locked.

Resigned, she sighed. "I guess the people there will talk to you better than they will me. But this is not an official request for help."

"Of course not." I grinned, the paper crackling against my skin.

"You tell me everything you discover, Kelly. Everything. I mean it."

"I promise."

Her shoulders drooped. "I guess it isn't enough for you that your brother and the man you love, not to mention your grandmother, have all been targeted by whoever is behind this?"

"I'm taking it into consideration, I'll be careful, but I won't back down. I'll fight for justice until the day I find my father's killer."

"I know." She pulled me into a rare hug. "I've grown to care for you. You're the daughter I'll never have. I don't want anything to happen to you."

"I kind of like breathing." I chuckled, trying to take the seriousness out of the situation. My mother had died when I was young. Dad and Ruthie had been my parents after her death. If Dad hadn't been murdered, Lori could have been my stepmother. A rush of warmth toward her rose in me, and I returned the hug.

She stepped back, keeping one hand on each of my shoulders. "Let's get these men back to the hospital, then go over the list and make a plan of attack for tomorrow."

"I'm not scheduled to be on the set until Monday."

She gave a sly smile. "With it being Sunday, few people will be around, and you can snoop without interruption. Questions can wait until the next day."

"That brain is why you're the cop and I'm the actress."

"And photographer. Don't forget your camera or Shutterbug. She's the best alarm system you could ask for."

I wouldn't forget either one.

After Morgan loaded the two injured men into the back of a dark-paneled van, I gave Brock one more kiss. "I'll see you in the morning."

"Guaranteed," he said. "You aren't going snooping without me."

"You're injured."

"I'm still walking and breathing. See you at breakfast." He tapped my nose. "Do not leave without me."

"Okay." I knew when I was beaten. I watched the van leave, then returned to the house to pore over the list with the others. Between Ruthie and me, we should know most of the names on the list.

"Oh." Ruthie pointed to a name on the list. "I'm going with you tomorrow. I'm looking for a new manager, and Hilga Smithwick might be just the one I need. She's ruthless."

"Awesome. What a great pretense to get the chance to question her."

Chapter Thirteen

Shutterbug and I arrived on the lot by eight a.m. I had no desire to do any snooping in the dark. Past such actions had proven unwise.

Not expecting anyone to be around other than a custodian or two, I left Shutterbug off her leash, put my camera around my neck, and headed for the studio head's trailer. Eric James Johnson III, most recent inheritor of the place, rarely showed his twenty-something face, and I seriously doubted I'd find any news in the trailer, but a girl had to start somewhere.

Using a set of lock picks Ruthie thought to be a humorous Christmas gift, I slipped inside easily enough. I made sure all the blinds were closed tight before turning on the light. The room contained a wall of faux-wood filing cabinets, a wooden desk, complete with desk blotter, lamp, and a mug full of pens and pencils. A leather chair invited a body to sit. The room looked like the office of an executive, but didn't look as if one existed. It resembled a photo of an office. Who ran the place if Johnson wasn't? There wasn't a single framed photo on the desk. No one used this office.

After snapping a couple of photos, I left the trailer, making sure the door locked behind me, and surveyed the large studio lot. I'd have to "borrow" a golf cart because I'd never cover as much space without one.

Luckily, I knew the custodian, Rod Looper, always left the key in the cart he used. Picking the lock on the maintenance shed didn't take long, and soon my dog and I were zipping across the lot toward…well, I had no idea. I'd know what to investigate when I saw it.

I parked the cart in front of the cafeteria. A side door hung open a good six inches. "We aren't alone here, girl." I patted Shutterbug's head. Since she didn't seem alarmed, I slid from the cart and into the building. "Hello?"

A scream ricocheted from my right. A loud clatter echoed.

"Dang, woman, you scared ten years off my life." Rod glared from around a trashcan. "What are you doing here?"

"I could ask you the same thing."

"I work here."

"Not on Sundays."

"I took Friday off, Miss Nosy, and have things to do." He glanced outside. "You stole a golf cart?"

"Borrowed." I grinned. No wonder my dog hadn't been concerned. She loved the grouchy custodian as evidenced by the dopey look on her face as he scratched behind her ears. "I'm investigating Robert Doyles' death."

"Of course you are. What do you need from me?"

This wasn't the first time Rod had offered to help. Sometimes it's the invisible people who work around us that know the most. "Anything you can give me." I pulled the list of suspects from my pocket. "Would any of these people have a reason to kill him?"

He scanned the paper. "My name isn't on there. I had a reason."

Shock rippled through me. "You aren't a killer."

"Most of those people aren't either, but they all have a motive. Because of that man, this studio almost folded. Imagine the fright that went through everyone who works here."

I pulled a chair away from one of the tables and sat down. "But enough to kill him? Seems like there should be something more."

He set the paper between us. "Let me look harder." For several minutes I stared at the bald spot on top of his head as he jotted notes next to names, or crossed them out. "There's no way Mary would kill anyone."

Mary, who worked in the cafeteria, seemed like one of the last genuinely kind people in Hollywood. I had to agree. "It is a rather long list."

"It won't be when I'm finished." He made a few more notes, then slid the paper over to me. "Down to five."

Well, it was a place to start. "Ruthie plans on

asking Hilga to represent her."

"Good luck with that. The woman's a harpy."

I noticed he put evil next to her name. "Her personality isn't a motive for murder, Rod."

"They had an argument a couple of days before he died. I got the impression they were…intimate, and he wanted to break if off."

Interesting. "Who's Lance Cruz?"

"New actor. Too big for his britches. I overheard him saying he'd loaned Doyles money."

Did the man owe everyone? Still, you couldn't get your money back if the one who owed you died. "My Lisa is not a killer."

He raised his eyebrows. "No? But I bet she can find out who is. Tell her to check all employee records for any person filing a formal complaint against the victim."

"Then she doesn't belong on the suspect list."

"I didn't put a check by her name, just didn't cross it off. If we're going to work together, you need to be less sensitive."

I hadn't realized we were working together. I thought I'd asked for a one-time moment of help. Reading down the list, I noted that other than Lance, most of the suspects were low-paid help such as cafeteria workers and those who were involved with the sets. My head jerked at seeing Louie's name. "Why do you think my director is a suspect?"

"It's no secret the two men hated each other, despite Doyles' financing of your show." He crossed his arms. "Did you know the two competed for the right to direct a show about twenty years ago, and Louie won out? Doyles said he paid off the judges. It took Louie a while to live that down. When Doyles threatened to pull his financing, it could be enough to send Louie over the edge."

That put Louie at the top of the list with Lana, Cheryl, and Rossi. "Thanks, Rod."

He smiled. "Anytime, kid. I like you. Be careful. You know bad people won't think twice about killing off a pretty little thing like you. I'll let you know if I learn anything else."

"Thank you, Rod, and I promise to return the golf cart when I'm finished."

"Make sure you do." He winked. "I know where you work." He stood and hefted the trash bag over his shoulder before whistling a tuneless melody on his way out the door.

I had seven solid suspects. Lana, Cheryl, Mildred, Hilga, Rossi, Cruz, and Louie. Not exactly a bunch of nobodies. Everyone except for Cheryl and Mildred were celebrities. It wouldn't be easy to question them without someone finding out.

"Boo!"

I whirled, fists up. "Susan Gilroy! Are you wanting to die today?" I glared at Shutterbug. Why hadn't she warned me about the approach of my nemesis?

"What are you doing here on a Sunday?" Her gaze flicked to the paper on the table.

"Rehearsing." I shoved the paper in my pocket. "What are you doing here?"

"Same thing you are. Doyles' death is big news. I want to solve it." She lifted her chin. "Then I'm going to write about his death."

She had me on every point. I did want to solve the murder *and* write a book.

"Want to work together?"

Why did everyone want to work with me? I was an actress, not a detective, although I did always get my guy or girl. "We'd kill each other before a day passed. Besides, you're paparazzi for a tabloid. No one is going to talk to you."

"Those wanting to earn a quick fifty bucks will." She crossed her arms.

"You're paying people?" I shook my head. "You're going to get crackpots, Susan. Every Tom, Dick, and Joe will tell you anything for fast money."

Her face fell. "I don't know of any other way to get people not to run when they see me and my cameraman coming. What happened to people wanting their fifteen minutes of fame? Larry is riding my rear to come up with something for the front page." Her shoulders slumped. "I got nothing."

Having lost a similar job, I felt sorry for her. Larry Richards, editor of the *Hollywood Tribune*, could be a harsh taskmaster. Maybe I could drop her a tidbit here and there. I tapped my right forefinger against my lips. What could I say that wouldn't jeopardize Lori's investigation?

The roar of a car engine came from behind the building.

"This sure is a busy place for a Sunday," Susan said.

Shutterbug's ears stood at attention. Her fur bristled.

"Come on. We need to get out of sight until we find out who it is."

I motioned for Shutterbug to follow as we ducked behind the food counter. I put a finger to my lips and peeked over the counter.

A tall woman with almost white hair, the shade called platinum, strolled through the back door. She glanced around the dining hall, paused, then turned and headed out the way she'd come. Rather than drive away, the crunch of gravel told us she walked away from the building.

"Who is that?"

Susan's eyes widened. "Seriously? That's Hilga Smithwick. She must be meeting with someone she represents. Not the nicest person, but we've no reason to hide from her."

"Other than the fact we have no good reason to be here on a Sunday?"

"Rehearsing, remember? I'm helping you by reading lines for you."

I shrugged. It seemed as good an excuse as any. "Let's follow her."

We darted out the door, staying far enough back so she couldn't hear our footsteps until she left the gravel area and moved to asphalt. We rounded one of the trailers. No sign of her. Ugh.

Shutterbug, nose to the ground, headed for a trailer across from where we stood. She turned around a few times, then stared at the trailer door. The slam of a car door had us ducking out of sight as Martin Rossi strode in our direction.

Chapter Fourteen

Martin yanked open the door to the trailer Hilga had entered, then slammed it behind him.

"Whose trailer?" Susan whispered.

"I have no idea. There's no name on the door." Which meant it could be unused at the moment. "Shh."

"I told you I have nothing to do with Robert's financial problems," Hilga said.

"You spent enough time with him. Where's the money hidden?" Rossi growled.

"Hidden?" Her voice rose. "You can't hide what you don't have. If he owes you money, then I'm sorry. He owed me plenty. Money, promises—you name it, and he promised it."

I widened my eyes at Susan. Hilga definitely sounded angry at Robert. Enough to kill him? I straightened to try and peer in the window. Being petite, I didn't stand a chance. "Give me a boost," I whispered.

Susan sighed and cupped her hands.

I stepped into them and pulled myself up, just enough to see inside. Hilga leaned on a small round table, looking as if she kept it between her and Rossi as a shield. She'd looked tough storming into the dining hall, but now she seemed frightened. Rossi appeared at ease in a straight-back chair as he dug under his fingernails with a pen knife.

"What do you want from me, Martin?"

"What I'm owed. You didn't complete the job I hired you for. Interest is piling up." He heaved a heavy sigh and stood. "I expect to see some money in one week, Hilga."

Job? Susan's hands trembled under me. I jumped to the ground and pulled her out of sight behind the trailer as the door opened.

Footsteps padded away, followed a few minutes later by the tapping of heels. I peeked from our hiding place in time to see Hilga round the cafeteria building.

"Come on." I grabbed Susan's hand. "You cannot print any of what we heard. Not until we have more facts."

She pulled free. "But, that's why I'm here."

"If you print it now, and one of them killed Doyles, you'll tip them off." I gripped her shoulders and shook her. "Have some sense."

"Fine. But once we have proof of something, I'm printing…." She marched toward the building.

Idiot. She'd put a target on her back. Mine, too, if anyone discovered I'd spied with her today.

Rossi stepped from behind a dumpster.

"Ladies." He tilted his head. While his voice sounded friendly, the hard glint in his eyes was not. How much had he heard?

"Mr. Rossi. What brings you out here today?" I forced a smile.

"I'm thinking of investing. You?"

"Rehearsing my lines."

His gaze flicked from me to Susan. "Without a script? Impressive."

"I left it in my trailer." I narrowed my eyes. "Wouldn't it make more sense for you to come see your potential investment when someone is here to show you around?"

"You're here." He reached for me, only to stop when Shutterbug growled and moved between us.

"Perhaps Mr. Johnson, or a custodian would be better for that job. Have a good day, Mr. Rossi." With my heart pounding in my throat, I rushed for my trailer, leaving Susan to follow. Once inside, I collapsed on the sofa.

"That is what you will face if you print their conversation."

"That's Martin Rossi, crime boss." She closed her eyes and took a deep breath. "How do you do it? Face killers without fainting?"

"Because I want justice served, and I've found I like writing true crime." I rubbed my hands down my face. "You have to treat suspects with a light hand. The last thing you want is a confrontation unless one, you have proof they're guilty, two…you're armed, and three…you aren't alone. We only had one of the three rules."

She sat next to me. "I act like a tough reporter,

but really I'm a coward."

"I won't think bad of you if you back away." How could I approach Hilga about the conversation without letting it slip that I'd eavesdropped?

"No, I'm not backing out. I could win a Pulitzer with this story."

"Is it worth potentially dying?" I doubted I could bring it up during an interview between her and Ruthie. I groaned. Having a conversation with myself *and* with Susan was giving me a headache.

"I'll have to make sure I don't die. After all, this is what…your fourth foray into crime solving? I'll just follow your lead."

"Great. I'm headed home. I'll let you know the next time I'm out and about."

She rolled her eyes. "I think I'll hang around the set tomorrow. Just in case you decide to snoop without me."

"What is she doing here?" Ruthie hissed, cutting a harsh glance to where Susan sat in a corner to watch the day's filming.

"She wants a story. Try to ignore her."

"Hard to do when the whole room reeks of her whorehouse perfume."

I sniffed. "I think that's you." I gave her a consoling pat on the shoulder and took my place on set. My gaze flicked to Louie. Once again, my director was a murder suspect. What did that say about my job choice?

"Focus, Canyon."

I jerked at his sharp command, then relaxed when I discovered his bark had been aimed at Ruthie who kept sniffing her armpits.

"Something wrong?" Louie's sarcastic tone cut through the room. "Somebody get this woman some deodorant!"

"I don't need any, thank you very much." Ruthie curled her lip and took her place behind the metal desk. "I'm ready. Do you like apricots?"

"That's not in the script." Louie flipped through the sheets of paper on his clipboard.

I palmed my forehead.

"I'm asking you a question," Ruthie said. "Not speaking my lines."

"Yes, I like them. Why?" He narrowed his eyes.

"What do you do with the pits?"

"Throw them away." He glanced at me. "What is wrong with her today?"

I shrugged. "I think she's getting senile."

"Take that back!" Ruthie bolted to her feet.

"Okay, she's awake now." I grinned and took my place behind the desk assigned to my character.

The room grew silent, then work resumed when no explosion came from Ruthie. The glare sent my way let me know we'd discuss my behavior later.

Ruthie didn't let me down. She chased after me all the way to the cafeteria when we took a lunch break. "Mind explaining your rude comment?"

"Would you mind telling me why you were baiting a suspect?"

"I'm trying to find out if he's capable of murder." She crossed her arms. "I can't work for someone who is, Kelly. It's outside my principles."

"Good grief, Grandma. Louie didn't kill anyone. Why would he?"

"He's on the list. He didn't like Robert. That's two reasons."

I laughed. "Nobody seems fond of Robert. That doesn't make them all killers. I'm going to focus on the women in his life."

"Can I put that in the paper?" Susan rushed toward us. "That doesn't give away too much information. I'll even say the police are looking at the women in his life to draw attention away from you."

"Don't mention any names. Now, if you two will give me some peace, I have a lunch date with Hollywood's most gorgeous."

"Lance Cruz?" Susan's eyes widened.

I frowned. "No, Brock." I hadn't met Lance yet, but his publicity photos showed an extremely handsome young man with dark blond hair and brooding hazel eyes. Still, nothing compared to Brock's dark hair and blue eyes. At least, not in my opinion.

I entered the cafeteria and scanned the room for Brock. Speak of the devil. Lance sat next to him. With a shrug, and ignoring the looks of young hopefuls around us, I joined the two leading men.

Brock stood. "Sweetheart, have you met Lance?"

"Not yet." I shook his hand. "Congratulations on your new role."

"Thanks." His soft voice rolled over me like a summer rain. Oh, he was going to be a big star. "I'm not a huge fan of kids, but playing a single dad whose child is kidnapped is kind of fun, actually. A twist on the mother who fights to rescue her child."

"I'm sure it will be a hit." I had so many questions. Did Brock invite the man to lunch with us to grill him or for less sinister reasons? He'd seen the suspect list. The big question in my mind was where did a brand, spanking-new actor get money to lend? I made a mental note to have Lisa do some research on Hollywood's newbie.

I excused myself and made a dash for my trailer. If I hurried, I'd make it back to the set on time and not suffer Louie's wrath. Lisa promised to have something by the end of the day.

I made it back to the set with minutes to spare and skid to a halt at the sight of Ruthie talking to Hilga. Not good. I needed to be there to monitor the conversation.

"Here she is." Ruthie smiled my way. "Kelly is also looking for an agent."

Hilga peered down her straight nose at me. "You are an up-and-coming star. I've heard good things about you."

"Thank you." She didn't sound impressed in the least. "Could we meet later over dinner?" I suggested. "Staletti's?"

She stared at me for a moment. "Seven o'clock." She clearly liked to be the one in control. I'd have to remember that and be more submissive. Even if Ruthie and I didn't end up with her as our agent, we needed to consider her until we proved her innocence or guilt. Thus we had some acting to do, or rather I did. Ruthie was ready to sign on the dotted line that second. I needed more time.

The possible agent slash manager gave me another stony look before leaving the set. Susan stared after her with wide eyes, clearly terrified the tall woman would notice her crouching in the corner.

"What is with that reporter?" Ruthie shook her head. "A couple of bolts loose, I think."

"She's in over her head. Let's get this filming over with. I want to see what Lisa dug up before we meet Hilga for dinner."

"We need to go home and change. We should look as stylish as she does." Ruthie entered the set made to look like a city street.

Tomorrow, the filming would take place on the actual street, but Louie wanted to run through some lines and still shots in front of a backdrop. A waste of time in my opinion, but hey, I got paid no matter how many times I said the same line.

When Louie finally released us, Ruthie and I hitched a ride to our trailer when Rod drove by in his golf cart. "See me tomorrow, Kelly." He tossed me a wink and dropped us off.

If we didn't already have plans for the evening, I'd follow him. Instead, I shoved open the door to the trailer. "Do you have something for me?"

Lisa nodded. "Of course I do. Have I ever failed you?"

"Make it snappy," Ruthie said. "We have to be somewhere in an hour and still need to change." She grabbed a handful of makeup-remover wipes and scrubbed at her face.

"Not so hard," Lisa said, frowning. "You'll cause more wrinkles."

"More?" Ruthie screeched, but softened her touch on her face.

"What did you find out?"

Lisa pulled her attention from Ruthie and back to her computer screen. "Not exactly a rags-to-riches story. Our dear boy, Lance, was adopted as an infant by a very wealthy family in Texas. He's got the money to loan Doyles. The records are sealed, so I don't know his birth name. He's never kept being adopted a secret, so it's possible he found out the information himself. I'll keep digging."

"But why? Lance just arrived on the scene. People don't lend money to strangers, do they?"

"This is Hollywood. People do all kinds of things."

"That's the truth." Ruthie tossed me the wipes. "Get busy. As for what people do, it's obvious Lance and Robert knew each other. You'll have to find out the connection. I'm not saying Lance wouldn't have lent the money if they didn't know each other well, but I am saying he would have a reason. Whether he was being nice, or there was something in it for him."

"Sometimes you surprise me with your brilliance," I said, giving her a quick kiss on the cheek.

She frowned. "Why? I'm brainy. Shouldn't be a surprise at all. Now hurry up. We cannot leave Hilga waiting. She'll drop us before the appetizers."

Chapter Fifteen

I donned a pair of wide-legged black pants and a royal blue sleeveless shirt. After fastening a wide belt around my waist and slipping my feet into a pair of black flats, I put my hair up into a quick twist and voilà, I was ready.

"At least put on some makeup, Kelly." Ruthie shook her head. "Five minutes."

Sighing, I dabbed on some powder, a quick dab of blush, a swipe of shadow and mascara and a tinted lip gloss. There. I made an effort. Shouldering a black purse, I hurried after Ruthie who wore a navy maxi skirt and a bright yellow, billowing blouse. Our styles couldn't be more different. She loved drama, I preferred simplicity. We complemented each other.

"Wonderful. We're ten minutes early." Ruthie hurried into the restaurant.

"Right this way," the hostess said, grabbing

three menus. "I'll lead Ms. Smithwick back when she arrives." She seated us in the fancier portion of the restaurant near a window.

"I'm so glad the girl sees the importance of ambiance during an important meeting." Ruthie smiled over her menu.

"Yes, that's very important." I returned her smile. "This means a lot to you, doesn't it?"

"Of course. She's the best in the business."

"What if she's our killer? I don't want you to be devastated like with Doug."

She slapped her menu on the table. "I was engaged to Doug, Kelly. It isn't the same thing at all."

Maybe not exactly, but I knew how set in her ways she could get. If she signed a contract with Hilga, she'd take it personally if the woman went to prison. She took a lot of things personally. "There she is."

I directed Ruthie's attention to where the hostess led Hilga to our table. The woman stared at the chair I sat in. She wanted me to move? Fine. I got up and moved to the right, giving her the seat that faced the door. I thought only cops had a thing about facing the door. No, wait, I was wrong. From the way Hilga's gaze kept flicking in that direction, she was looking for someone.

"Are you expecting someone else?" I asked.

"Of course not. I never double-book." She opened her menu.

I glanced at Ruthie, silently asking, "Are you sure you want this woman as your manager?"

She didn't get the clue. "I recommend the

lasagna," my grandmother gushed. "Special sauce. Leo refuses to divulge the recipe."

"I'll be eating a salad." Hilga never pulled her gaze away from the menu until she'd made her choice. Then, she closed it and snapped her fingers to get the waitress's attention.

"Great. I wasn't finished looking at the menu, but I'll have the chicken gnocchi, with a house salad." I pressed my lips together.

Ruthie kicked me under the table. "That's your favorite."

"I'll be hungry again in two hours."

Hilga narrowed her eyes. "I've heard Ruthie is high-maintenance, but I expected you to be easier to work with."

"High-maintenance?" Ruthie clutched her throat, her chin trembling. "Someone told you that?"

"Of course." Hilga shrugged one elegant shoulder. "I do my homework before meeting with a potential client."

At least the description of Ruthie hadn't turned her off…yet. "My apologies, Hilga. We had a rough day of filming. I shouldn't let it affect my attitude." Liar. I didn't like to be lorded over, and tended to retaliate in kind.

The waitress arrived with our salads, Ruthie choosing the lighter fare so as not to be left out, then left and returned again with my soup. Leo smiled in our direction as he passed through the room. His smile seemed a bit stilted as it landed on Hilga, and he didn't stop.

"How strange." Ruthie's gaze followed him.

"Since I've hired him to cater my wedding, you'd think he'd at least come and say hello."

"You're getting married?" Hilga's brows rose. "When?"

Ruthie waved her left hand with the large diamond on her ring finger. "Not for a few months. Why?"

"Keep it low scale. You're too old for a big event."

Ouch. Ruthie's eyes filled with tears.

I reached under the table and took her hand, giving it a gentle squeeze. "Ruthie will have the wedding she wants."

"Don't say I didn't warn you when people begin to talk." Hilga set down her fork. "I've already decided to take on the two of you, but I have a few requirements."

Here we go. I peered up at her over my spoon, then straightened at Ruthie's stern look. Fine. I'd give her highness my full attention and let my soup grow colder.

"It's no secret how you are always in the tabloids, which can be a good thing," Hilga said, "but I'd rather it be industry-related than you almost get yourself killed. Bad publicity. You've gotten a reputation, Kelly, as Hollywood's pit bull."

"Really?" I grinned. "I take that as a compliment."

She folded her hands on the table, closed her eyes, and I'm pretty sure she counted to ten before looking at me. "You are a beautiful, petite lady and should act like one. Stop wearing jeans and chambray shirts everywhere you go. Fix your hair.

You do look nice tonight, though."

I crossed my arms. "Stop being myself, you mean."

"You are selling yourself every time you step foot outside."

"What about me?" Ruthie's voice trembled. She obviously hadn't gotten over the age comment.

"You're perfect, other than finding roles being more difficult because of your age. Still, you've taken care of yourself and you look years younger." She gave Ruthie a thin-lipped smile.

"I suppose I should be grateful for that." A spark ignited in my grandmother's eyes.

I grinned and settled back to watch the show, sneaking a spoonful of my soup when I could get away with the act.

"You don't think my granddaughter, who won an award, by the way, or myself, who's won several, are fine the way we are? I realize Doug Lincoln was a crook, but he managed to get us good jobs despite his moral character. Now, here you are telling us we need to change in order to keep working? Am I hearing you right?" A blotch formed on Ruthie's neck.

Hilga gave a long sigh. "The industry is changing, ladies. You need to keep up. Also, I would suggest that Ruthie get unengaged because she's believed to be in a relationship with a leading man, and Kelly should spread herself around a little and not be seen only with Brock Hanson."

"That's it." Ruthie tossed her napkin on the table and stood. "And I thought you were the manager I wanted. I was wrong. Good day, Ms.

Smithwick."

Her eyes widened. "You're turning *me* down?"

"Most definitely. You see…." Ruthie gave a shark-like grin, "I, too, had second thoughts. Your reputation as an adulteress and murder suspect precede you." With a toss of her hair over her shoulder, she stormed away.

"Murder suspect?" Hilga cast me a questioning look. "Where in the world did that idea come from?"

"Did you kill Robert Doyles?" I continued eating. No need to impress the woman now.

"Of course not."

"But you were hired to keep tabs on him, right? Act as a girlfriend?"

Her brows lowered. "Where do you find your information?"

"That little tidbit I overheard myself. Did you care for him or not?"

"I couldn't stand the man. Self-absorbed and an idiot. But, he could be fun on occasion, and I did enjoy our trips to Europe."

"Is that where his money is?"

She slammed her hands on the table. "There is no money. What is with everyone thinking he hid some away. Robert has a secret, one I didn't have a chance to uncover, but I'm pretty certain he died a financially broken man." She pushed to her feet and leaned close to me. The pungent smell of Italian salad dressing tickled my nose. "You do not want to get on the wrong side of Rossi." She seized her purse and left me to finish eating alone.

Hilga hadn't denied working for Rossi, and her

threat at the end of the conversation confirmed she knew the man. Of course, after seeing them talking. I also felt it a reasonable assumption that he frightened her. We agreed on that point. Rossi scared me spitless.

I also discovered an interesting piece of information. Robert had a secret outside of money. Another woman to add to a long line of lovelies, or was it something else? My bet was on something else. If I figured out what, I might find his killer.

After I finished my dinner, I paid the bill and went searching for my grandmother. I found her leaning against a column in the outdoor garden area. "You okay?" I put a hand on her shoulder.

"I don't like that woman, but yes, I'm fine." She sniffed.

"Are you crying?"

"Having a bit of a pity party as I sip my wine." She held up an almost empty glass. "My second. I'm having a hard time dealing with growing older. I know I've held up well, as that rotten woman said, but age isn't something I can hold at bay. I've relied on my beauty my entire life."

"You're still beautiful." I put my arm around her shoulder. "That's not something that can be taken away from you. Not to mention how proud I am of you for putting that woman in her place. Well done."

A smile teased her lips. "I was rather fierce, wasn't I? I won't allow anyone to get between me and Mark. No one."

"Morgan is definitely the perfect man for you." Not many would put up with her diva side.

Ruthie pulled out a wrought-iron chair and sat down. "Did you get any information from her?"

I sat across from her and motioned for the waitress to bring us two glasses of iced tea. "She didn't deny working for Rossi, definitely didn't like Robert, and said he had a secret she couldn't solve."

"I like that." She frowned at the tea. "I'd prefer wine, dear."

"Nope. Two is enough. Have another when you get home if you want. I'm not driving around town with a drunken granny."

"You're a cruel child." She sighed. "I should've paid attention to the tales of Hilga and saved us a deplorable dinner. We could have spent the evening with our men."

"It wasn't a total waste. You put her in her place. I doubt that's been done before."

She giggled. "It felt wonderful, and she stays on our suspect list."

"Yep, right along with Lana, Cheryl, Mildred, Rossi, and Lance. It's ridiculous to think Louie could kill someone. He just acts tough. The next person I want to try and rule out is Mildred. She doesn't seem likely either."

Ruthie twirled her tea glass. "I guess that would depend on how devoted to Lana she is."

"More than a housekeeper?"

"Why else would she hang around like a watchdog every time we're there? She's protecting her or wants to know everything that is said, or both."

I sipped my tea and stared out over the small water feature. Plausible, but something about that scenario bothered me. She'd grown up with Morgan, and he was an excellent judge of character. If Mildred were shady, he'd have picked up on it, right?

"What are you thinking?"

"I want to talk to Morgan about Mildred before we question her."

"Oh."

"Jealous?" I smiled.

"Not even a little. The woman is a plain Jane."

"Looks aren't everything."

"They've worked for me all these years." She laughed. "I'm rather in love with myself, aren't I?"

"Just a little." I stood. "Ready to go home?"

"Definitely."

As we stood to leave, the window in front of us shattered.

Chapter Sixteen

I tackled Ruthie to the ground as screams rang out. Something soaked through my shirt. Had I been shot? I waited for pain more severe than the shards of glass piercing the palms of my hands. Nothing. I put a hand to my side. It came away clear. A glance at the table behind me showed spilled tea. *Thank you, Lord.* "Ruthie?"

"What happened?" She struggled to her feet.

"I think someone took a shot at us." Sirens wailed in the distance.

"Wonderful." She grinned and limped to the wall where she hovered in its shelter. "That means we know something we don't know we know. We're getting close."

"That's one way of putting it." Usually meant we were getting too close. I sat next to her and frowned at a tear in the leg of my pants. I loved these pants.

Leo shoved through the crowd to reach us. "You alright?"

"We're fine. This is becoming the norm for us."

He glowered. "Not for me. I want that window fixed."

"I'll fix it," Ruthie said with a scowl.

"Not by you. By whoever threw that rock."

"Rock?" Ruthie and I said in unison.

"It wasn't a bullet?" I got to my feet.

He stepped through the broken window and retrieved a rock wrapped in a brown bag. "There's one word written on it in black marker. *Warned.* Better than a bullet, I guess."

"Definitely." I took the rock from him and gently set it on the table. "Don't go anywhere. You'll have to be fingerprinted."

"Already on file." He smirked. "I was a wild kid."

He regaled us with tales of wild car chases, stealing whiskey from his father's pub, and shooting birds off fences with a BB gun until Lori and Jason arrived. "Now that the two of you are in good hands, I'll go entertain the others while they wait their turn to be interrogated."

"One day of peace, Kelly." Lori glared down at me.

"It's not my fault I can't have dinner with my grandmother. Hey, good news is it was just a rock."

She didn't seem impressed, but did she glance at it as Jason dropped it into a bag. "Are either of you hurt?"

"Nope, but a glass of wine wouldn't hurt. Might take the sting out of these pricks." Ruthie waved at a waitress.

I decided to let my previous no go unchallenged. I'd curb her drinking when we got home. "Just cuts from the glass, a skinned knee, nothing drastic."

Lori righted a chair I'd knocked over as I knelt next to Ruthie. "Tell me what happened," Lori said.

I told her of our dinner, Ruthie's smackdown of Hilga, then our coming out here. "Throwing a rock might be something Hilga would do. Someone more aggressive, a man maybe, might use a gun."

"Don't accuse without evidence." She did circle Hilga's name though, which meant she agreed with me. A warmth of pleasure traveled through me.

"What do you know about Mildred? I mean, if she grew up with Morgan, you had to have known her."

Her brow furrowed. "They're older than me. I didn't hang out with their group. Besides, I'm asking the questions here. You can bother Morgan later."

"Thanks for giving me permission." I gave her a cheeky grin.

A smile tugged the corner of her lips. "I'm glad the two of you are okay. Go home. I'll see you later. Wait a minute. Where is my brother? The two of you are supposed to have a bodyguard."

Ruthie raised her hand. "He's locked in the bathroom; well, he's probably out by now. I wanted to meet with Hilga alone. I can't have my fiancé thinking he'll be with me twenty-four-seven. I'm a modern woman, and he needs to accept that."

"You locked him in the bathroom?" I didn't

think it possible for Lori's eyes to widen further, but they did. "He's going to strangle you."

"Then we'll see you at the murder scene."

"Look." Lori stood. "I understand independence, but stupidity? I don't care where you're going or who you see, do not go without Morgan. Understand?"

Ruthie nodded, resigned. "Sure, I'll keep him on a leash."

Lori whirled to face me. "I expected more from you."

"We're in a public place."

"A lot of good that did."

"Morgan can't be two places at once. Ruthie and I are not always together."

"Then have your dog or Brock with you." She tossed her hands up and stomped away.

"Wow, what a temper." Ruthie finished her wine. "Ready?"

"She has a point," I said as we made our way to the car. "Both of us tend to forget about the danger because of the excitement." We'd long ago confessed to each other that getting involved in mysteries was our own particular drug.

She nodded, sliding into the passenger seat. "We'd best go console Mor—oh, there he is."

Morgan, every line in his body rigid, strode toward us. He climbed into the backseat without a word and crossed his arms.

"I'm sorry, sweetie." Ruthie batted her lashes.

No response. Not even the blink of an eye.

I decided to wait until he settled down before questioning him about Mildred.

At home, he took Ruthie by the arm and led my subdued grandmother to the bedroom. I met Sarah's curious gaze. I shrugged. "She needs a spanking." I followed and pressed my ear to the door. A dangerous thing to do with most people, but there'd be no hanky-panky going on. I just wanted to make sure neither of them lost their temper, in case I needed to barge in and rescue someone. Morgan would never raise a hand to my grandmother, but I couldn't say the same about her.

Sarah squeezed next to me. "I can't hear anything."

"I'm pretty sure they're having a glaring contest. You'll hear the shouting in a few minutes."

The front door opened, and Brock entered the house. He glanced over, grinned, and joined us. "What are we doing?"

I quickly filled him in on the evening's events.

"You haven't cleaned up your cuts." His gaze roamed over me.

"I will later. Shh."

"What were you thinking?" Morgan broke the silence. "Of all the idiotic, selfish, unthink—"

"I've already heard it from your sister. I don't need a repeat."

"Why, Ruthie?"

"I wanted some independence, I guess."

"We're getting married." His voice softened. "We'll be together a lot. Are you having second thoughts?"

Things hadn't escalated as I'd thought they would. Instead, they'd turned personal. "Come on. They need to work this out."

Brock took my hand. "Go put on some clean clothes, and I'll doctor your cuts."

When I joined him in the kitchen ten minutes later, Morgan and Ruthie were already there. From the soft, goo-goo glances, they'd made up and come to an understanding.

Brock hefted me onto the counter as if I were a child. "Let me do this."

Okay. I wasn't one to push away caring ministrations from a handsome man.

Brock's dark head bent over my skinned knee. He gently pressed a cloth covered in a burning antiseptic against my skin, then blew on the wound. He smiled up at me and placed a kiss before sticking on a Band-Aid.

My heart raced. Only this man could make wiping away blood sexy enough to take a woman's breath away. I swallowed, my mouth as dry as cotton and forgot there were others in the room. I gripped him by the hair and pulled him to his feet. "Kiss me."

He obliged, wrapping his arms around my waist and pulling me close. "All you have to do is ask," he murmured against my lips.

Someone cleared their throat, ripping me back to the kitchen. My face heated as Brock chuckled and returned to caring for the cuts on my palms.

Despite the late hour, after our wounds were tended to, we gathered in the living room for coffee. I filled the men in on Lori's warning and added my apology to Ruthie. "I seriously didn't think we'd be in danger at Staletti's. It won't happen again."

"Do you feel suffocated with all of us under the

same roof?" Morgan asked.

I shook my head. "The more the merrier. Every night is a party." I smiled, leaning my head on Brock's shoulder. "We've plenty of room. If I want privacy, I'll go to my studio or my bedroom. With each of us having our own space, it isn't a problem."

"I'm the kink in the rope," Ruthie said, "but it's just wedding jitters. I'll be fine."

Since everyone had mellowed, I thought it a good time to ask Morgan about his childhood friend. "How well did you know Mildred? What's her last name?"

"Carson. I knew her pretty well. She lived next door. Followed me and my friends around as long as we'd let her. Sometimes she joined in a baseball game. She was good, for a girl." He winked at Ruthie.

"Did she have any siblings?"

"A sister, and a brother with multiple sclerosis. He passed away when we were in high school." He balanced his elbows on his knees. "Why all the questions, Kelly? I don't think she's capable of murder."

"She seems overly protective of Lana."

"Maybe that's her job."

I shrugged. "Maybe, but she seems intense to me. As if she's afraid Lana will say something she shouldn't."

"Maybe she is." His gaze pierced mine. "Lana hid money from her husband and she's been seen with a notorious crime boss. Mildred might be afraid of losing her job."

"Or she's being paid to keep an eye on Lana. I can't see Rossi letting Lana have much freedom."

He frowned and sat back. "That's a thought I hadn't considered. You might be onto something."

"How would I approach her about the topic? You know her better than anyone else here."

"I guess I'll go with you. Tomorrow?"

"We wrap up filming for the season, so right afterward would be great. Then," I glanced at Ruthie, "we have a trip to Vegas to plan, unless we find out something that clears up our suspicions about Rossi." Somehow, I thought we'd have more questions than answers after speaking to Mildred. "I want to keep a close eye on Hilga also. It's too much of a coincidence that a warning would be thrown through the very restaurant window we were at so soon after she left."

"I agree," Brock said. "Have you asked Lisa to look into her yet?"

"No, I didn't have a lot of reasons other than her connection to Rossi. This mystery gets more and more tangled. We have gambling, adultery, secrets…"

"It'll click into place eventually." Brock gave me a one-armed hug. "It always does. Just don't run off and leave me hanging like the last time."

Sarah patted his shoulder as she gathered up the coffee mugs. "I took good care of your girl, didn't I?"

"You sure did." He grinned up at her. "You knew Robert as well or better than any of those people. Who do you think killed him?"

"I'm not sure. There is one thing I've suspected

for a long time, though. I think he has a child out there no one knew about. Maybe that's your killer."

The room silenced as we all stared at her. A secret child? Could that be what Hilga had worked at discovering? "Why do you say that?"

"Because I found a photo of a newborn. One of those ones they take at the hospital. I couldn't tell whether it was a boy or a girl, though. The baby wore a red onesie. Robert had no family, so why have a photo of a baby hidden in a secret drawer of his desk?" She raised her eyebrows. "That's right. When I suspected him of cheating, I snooped, but I never got to confront him. I put the photo back. The next day, he packed up his things, including the picture, and left."

"Who was he involved with before you?"

She gave a sarcastic laugh. "As many people as possible." She whipped around and headed for the kitchen. "Find out the identity of that baby, and I bet you'll find a clue to his killer," she said over her shoulder.

Chapter Seventeen

I doubted we'd find the name of a secret baby, but we converged on Lana's house anyway. By we, I mean, me, Ruthie, and Morgan. No way was my grandmother being left behind. A good excuse for being there evaded me.

Instead, we stood on the porch with no plan and waited for Mildred to answer the door so we could ask her enough questions to scratch her off our suspect list. While Ruthie rang the doorbell, I glanced around the manicured lawn. Lana didn't seem to have let the landscapers go. The freshly-cut lawn was as pristine as the last time we'd been there. How much money had she squirreled away? It had to cost a fortune to run a house the size of the one she lived in.

The door opened, and Mildred's gaze locked on Morgan as if Ruthie and I weren't there. It wasn't until my grandmother cleared her throat that the woman glanced our way. Her smile dipped a bit, but she stepped back and let us in. "Lana is getting ready for the day. It takes her a while."

"That's okay," I said. "We're here to see you too."

"Me?" She put a hand to her chest. "Whatever for?"

"Let's sit, Millie." Morgan led her to the sofa.

"Millie?" Ruthie scrunched up her face. "I think these two were more than friends once upon a time."

I was beginning to get the same impression. "Shh." We joined them in the living room.

Mildred's hands fidgeted on her lap as she sat where I guessed she rarely got invited to. "Let me at least get Cheryl to serve refreshments."

"She's not a great chef." Morgan smiled and put his hand over hers. "We'll pass, unless it's water."

She bit her lip to hold back a smile. "I can get your water."

"I'll get it. Don't start without me." I wanted to see firsthand that nothing was added to any of our glasses.

No sign of Cheryl at the sink or the stove, so I opened cabinets until I found four glasses. Inside the fridge was a pitcher of water which I left where it was and used the water dispenser in the corner of the room instead. I wasn't taking any chances. After I added ice, I found a tray to carry the drinks on, and returned to the others.

"Here you go. Something palatable." I set the tray on the coffee table and glanced up to see Cheryl's wounded expression. "Sorry."

"I wouldn't be a chef if I didn't know how to cook." She lifted her chin.

"You're a chef in this house because of Robert, not because you have any skill," Mildred said. "Sit down and keep quiet. I'm sure these nosy people want to ask you questions too. Shall we wait for Lana?"

"I didn't realize I'd invited guests for breakfast." Lana, her bruises faded, hovered in the doorway. She seemed paler than usual under impeccably applied makeup. "My apologies if I've forgotten."

"No, we're just here to talk." Ruthie ushered her to her lounge. "Are you doing better, you know, since the funeral?"

"I'm surviving. Thank you for asking." She reclined against the chair and laid an arm across her eyes. Dramatic? "Cheryl, why do I not have my glass of morning tomato juice?"

"I was getting it before I was interrupted." Cheryl lunged to her feet and raced for the kitchen.

"Why do you keep her as your chef?" I sat next to Ruthie. "It's obvious you don't care for her, she was your husband's mistress, and she has no talent in the kitchen."

Lana peered from under her arm. "Robert left a document saying I couldn't fire her or Mildred."

I glanced at the older woman. "Why you?"

Mildred shrugged. "I've been his housekeeper for a long time. I'm guessing he wanted to make sure I was cared for." Her words held little warmth for the man.

"But what if Lana can't pay you?"

Mildred gave a long exhale. "He thought of that."

Lana cleared her throat and crossed her long legs. "Look. My husband had a gambling problem. That is no longer a secret. So, while his money is gone, the money he set aside to pay…these two women is not."

"Robert grew a conscience after his divorce with Sarah?" Morgan leaned back against the sofa.

"I suppose."

"Did he leave you money?" I asked.

"Those types of questions will get me in trouble."

Okay, so he did have a fund for her. In addition to what she'd squirreled away…wait a minute. Rossi had to suspect there were hidden accounts. And he'd want that money to pay off Robert's debt. "Why don't you hand it over to Rossi and get him off your back?"

"I can't touch the accounts with Cheryl's and Mildred's names on them."

Nor did she want to give up what she'd worked hard for. Being married to the man couldn't have been easy.

Cheryl returned with a glass of tomato juice and a stalk of celery. "Robert wants me to use my fund for schooling."

"Culinary?" Ruthie looked hopeful.

"No, I want to be a makeup artist on horror films."

I didn't see that coming. "I'm going to ask a question, and I want all three of you to blurt out the first name that comes to your lips. Ready?" All three heads nodded. "Who do you think killed him?"

Lana and Mildred said Cheryl's name. The chef blurted out Mildred. I thought at least one of them would have mentioned the crime lord.

"If two of you suspect Cheryl, why is she still working here?" I narrowed my eyes. "I'd have found a way to get around the contract if I suspected someone of murder."

"She hasn't tried to kill us," Lana said. "Why make waves? I have enough to deal with." She sipped at her drink.

"Cheryl, why did you say Mildred's name?"

"Have you seen the way she stares at Lana?" She stretched out her arm and pointed. "It's as if she's waiting for her to die, watching every move she makes so she can pounce."

"Oh, don't be ridiculous." Mildred scowled. "I'm just conscientious enough to make sure all of my boss's needs are met."

"Whatever." Cheryl climbed to her feet. "I've work to do. Any other questions you want to ask that aren't any of your business?"

I smiled. "Nope." The chef would remain on my suspect list, alongside Mildred and Lana. "We'll be leaving now. Thank you for the…water."

Lana waved toward the door. "Mildred, see them out. I'm not feeling well."

"What's new?" she muttered.

Back at the car, I turned to Morgan and Ruthie. "I can't imagine sharing a house with someone I hated, much less two of them. Those women are not friends."

"Mildred isn't the Millie I used to know." Morgan climbed into the back seat. "The last time I spoke to her, she still had the softness of the young girl I grew up with. Now, she has a hardened edge that makes her a stranger. I need to look into what's happened to her since we were teenagers."

"Great idea. Lisa is digging around the internet on the three of them." I turned the key in the ignition and circled back to the highway.

"Next stop Vegas?" Ruthie asked, her voice full of hope.

"I don't think we need to." I glanced in the rearview mirror at Morgan. "Do you? I still have a hard time thinking Rossi would have killed Robert. There's no way to get money from a dead person."

"I agree. For now, Vegas is off the table."

"Darn." Ruthie flopped in her seat. "I do love the casino."

"Since when?" I shot her a look.

"Since forever. There's something about the lights and the sounds…" she sighed. "I just love it. Come on. We've finished filming and have the time. If not to investigate, then let's go have fun. Just for the weekend."

I grinned. "Fine. Let's go to Vegas." I'd have to let Brock and Lisa know. I'd promised my makeup artist I'd take her, and I didn't want to go without my man.

After we arrived home, I gave them a call. Brock would pack and be over after. Lisa promised to meet us bright and early in the morning. I left making reservations up to Ruthie. Now that plans were being made, excitement started to build.

After months of filming, often long days, it'd be nice to leave everything behind and play. I actually packed a party dress in case Brock and I could slip away to somewhere fancy.

Sarah stepped into my room. "Are you taking the dogs? Because if you aren't, I know someone who can watch them."

"Of course, we're taking the dogs." Ruthie frowned, passing the room. "They're service animals. The hotels have to allow them in. Plus, I know people."

"True. She'll convince whoever is in charge to let us in. Go pack and stop worrying."

"I can't help but worry. Vegas is what got Robert in trouble to start with." She left me alone to sort through more clothes than I'd need for a weekend away. I didn't even like clothes that much, and here I was trying to decide between two different blue shirts.

"What's bothering you?" Ruthie asked as she lingered at the door.

"I'm not sure." I dropped the shirts on the bed and sat down, flopping back across the mattress. "I think it's the fact I'm clueless."

"I could have told you that." She laughed and sat next to me, the mattress giving a little under her weight. "The pieces will fall into place. You'll see or hear something that will make everything click."

"Something is clicking, but not into place." The names and faces of my suspects swirled in my head. Maybe I did need the craziness of Vegas to settle things down. "Slap me if you catch me thinking about this case over the weekend."

"Oh, goody." Ruthie patted my leg, then moved to the door. "Wear the spaghetti strap under that black lace shrug. You have nice shoulders."

Maybe I should have her pack for me. I finished rolling clothes into the small suitcase. For good measure, I shoved my gun into the netted pouch.

"That's supposed to be in your purse." Ruthie said on her way past my room again.

"Are you spying on me?" I peered out my door. "What in the world has you running back and forth?"

"I haven't gotten my ten thousand steps in yet today. I started doing that on Monday. It's supposed to be good for the heart. You should try it."

"I jog." I started to withdraw, then stopped. "Don't tell Brock I keep forgetting my gun."

"I won't, because *you* just did." She laughed as he came up the stairs, a frown between his blue eyes.

"Kelly."

"I know. I'm a lost cause, but I hate carrying a purse, and sometimes there's no room left in my camera bag." I gave him a quick kiss.

"I hope you never need it."

"I always have my pepper spray and stun gun." I took his hand and pulled him into the room. "Talk to me while I finish packing. Where's Brutus?"

"Chasing Sassy while your wise dog watches. Where are we staying that allows dogs?"

"Ruthie is handling it."

"Bad news." Speaking of the devil. "I've had to rent a house on the outskirts of the strip. Never seen it. No idea what condition it's in, but not even I could get someone to let two large dogs, plus a little yapper, stay in their hotel. Fiends." She stomped away.

Brock laughed. "It'll be an adventure."

"All we'll do is sleep and shower there. It'll be fine." I'd lived under a bridge for a couple of weeks, so how bad could a rental be?

Chapter Eighteen

"**They should have** posted pictures." Ruthie clutched Sassy to her chest. "This place doesn't look safe. This is where the dumb blond in movies is killed by the psycho in a mask."

She was right. The ramshackle, pink-stucco house, miles from the strip, looked ready to fall down. Thick bushes and low-hanging tree branches kept the house in shadow. I expected an axe-wielding maniac to greet us. "This is the last time you make reservations." At least the place had a chain-link fence around the postcard-size yard to keep the animals contained.

"We might as well go in. This is our home for the next two nights." Morgan hefted a suitcase in each hand and shoved open the front door. "I'll protect you from Jason, Freddy, Michael, and other slash-and-gore monsters."

Chipped-tile floor, threadbare furniture, two

bedrooms, a closet of a kitchen, and one bathroom made up the house where we'd be staying. "Why don't the rest of you go to a hotel, and I'll stay here with the dogs." I could sacrifice when I needed to. Too many people for too small a house.

"No, I'm the one who rented this place," Ruth said. "I should be the one to stay here."

"We'll rent cots, crowd into the two bedrooms, and we'll all stay." Brock grinned. "It'll be fun. An adventure."

I loved his sense of adventure. Brock could find the good in almost anything. "Great." I rubbed my hands together. "Let's fill this dorm-sized refrigerator with the food we brought, get sleeping arrangements organized, and hit the strip."

After a trip to the store for foldaway cots, some clever maneuvering of said cots in the tiny bedrooms, then jostling for time in the bathroom, we finally hailed a ride to the glitz and glamour that was the Vegas strip.

Ruthie glowed as bright as a slot machine in a hot-pink, sequined dress. She shouldn't be hard to keep an eye on, but she melded into the background the moment we entered the casino. I didn't envy Morgan his job. Linking my arm through Brock's, I let him lead me to the roulette table. An hour into our play time, the table grew quiet. I turned to see the attraction.

Rossi, a beautiful woman on each arm, approached. He nodded in my direction, but continued through the casino and into an elevator. I shouldn't have been surprised to see him. After all, he lived in the city, but I thought maybe I'd get lucky enough to have a normal evening with no sign of murder suspects.

"Relax, sweetheart." Brock placed a bet. "He can't bother you in a crowded casino."

"Have you ever heard about disappearing in plain sight?" I missed the bet because I still stared at the elevator doors. A good thing, because I saw Hilga step into the elevator a few minutes later. The suspense was killing me. "I have to know what's going on."

"High stakes poker on the next level," the dealer said. "The game is by reservation only, but anyone can watch if they pay the fifty-dollar cover charge."

I glanced at Brock who gave a reluctant nod. He swept his chips into his hands and headed for the cashier box. "You sure know how to ruin a winning streak."

"Sorry, but we might find out what Hilga's up to."

"Poker."

"I mean in regard to the murder." I rolled my eyes. "Maybe she'll say something about the rock thrown through Staletti's window."

We didn't make it far before we were surrounded by pretty young women in tight, low-cut dresses that barely covered their rear ends, their faces made up and hair styled. Being a good sport, Brock autographed whatever they wanted him to, short of body parts best covered up.

I shifted from foot to foot. At this rate, we'd miss Hilga talking to Rossi.

Brock finally broke free from the throng, cashed in his chips, then we made a beeline for the elevators. He smiled and waved, pressing the button to close the doors before any of the starry-eyed girls could join us.

"I bet they'll still chase after you when you're sixty," I said.

"Will that bother you?"

I grinned. "Not as long as you're still with me." I hugged his arm. It did something to a girl's ego to be on the arm of the most gorgeous man around.

The doors opened onto a mezzanine. Thick, burgundy carpet muffled our footsteps as we followed the well-dressed people through a set of glass doors. Brock paid the cover fee for each of us, and we took our seats behind a glass partition.

On a platform a few feet below us were Rossi, Hilga, and two other men I didn't know. They sat around a round table, stacks of chips in front of them. A man in a dark suit announced that the spectators must remain quiet at all times. There went any chance of me learning any information. Except… I leaned closer as the game progressed.

Hilga and Rossi might be seated across from each other, but it seemed as if there were secret glances and hand signals between them that the other two players were unaware of. "They're cheating," I whispered.

The dark-suited man put a finger to his lips.

I jerked my head toward the table. When he didn't catch on to what I was trying to tell him, I sighed and crossed my arms. Hilga was definitely helping Rossi win, and the stack of chips in front of the man continued to grow.

Hilga glanced up and caught sight of me, then

signaled to Rossi. He peered over his shoulder and glared, eyes narrowing.

Time to go. I grabbed Brock's hand. As we passed the man in the suit, I whispered that they were cheating, then ducked out the door.

"What if he tells Rossi you snitched?" Brock yanked me to a halt. "Did you forget whom we're dealing with?"

"No. I'm trying to flush a rat out of the sewer." I caught sight of two muscled men exiting the poker room. "Time to go." I kept a firm grip on Brock's hand and took off at a run.

"I'll never understand how women can run in heels," Brock said as we darted into the stairwell.

"Practice." We thundered to the first floor and exploded back into the crowded casino. There we could blend in with the crowd much easier.

"Let's go somewhere else and get something to eat," Brock suggested. "Wait for things to cool down some, maybe go to a different casino. I'll text Morgan and let him know. He can gather the others."

"I'd rather let them know, but eat alone. We don't get to do that often." I smiled. "In fact, I'd like to order a pizza, head back to the shack, and spend a quiet evening with us and the dogs. Let the others play."

His gaze heated. "I like that idea. We can eat fancy tomorrow."

Less than an hour later, dressed in tee-shirts and shorts, we sat in rickety lawn chairs on the concrete slab intended as a patio in the backyard. We munched on pizza while the dogs cast hopeful glances for a piece of crust thrown their way. Away from the strip, the night sounds reached us. Birds settling down in the trees, a cat protesting on the other side of the fence, the murmur of a couple in the house next door as they worked in their yard.

Back home, the sprawling mansions were too far apart to hear neighbors. I think I preferred it that way and kept my voice low as I talked with Brock. "Why do you think Rossi cheated?"

"To gain back some of what he lost?" Brock wiped his mouth with a paper napkin.

"But the man is supposed to be loaded. Would it be that much of a hardship for him to lose…what? How much are we talking about?"

"No idea, but it must be a big chunk for all the fuss. It takes a few million to produce a television show. What if he borrowed more than just to cover his gambling debt?"

"Maybe." I stretched my legs out in front of me and crossed my ankles. "Something still seems off. I think we're dealing with two separate issues. Robert's gambling debt to Rossi and his murder. I'm starting to think they aren't linked."

"The common factor being Doyles."

Brock drummed his fingers on the arm of the chair. "Rossi, Hilga, Lana, Robert, all connected by money. One of them killed him, maybe not because of money, but something else. What? A secret child? What's the motive?"

"Hmmm." I stared into the night sky. "The child could be mad because he'd been given away. The mother could be angry because Robert abandoned her and the child. Neither seem strong enough of a motive to kill, but then I'm not a psycho."

He gave my hand a squeeze. "That's debatable."

"Oh, hush." I turned my head and smiled. The moon highlighted his dark hair with strands of silver. "You're so handsome. Thank you for not being conceited about your looks."

He laughed. "You have no idea how beautiful you are."

"I'm just the girl next door who cleans up nice."

He pulled me close, his lips a breath away. "Real nice." He kissed me. "Thank you for the great idea of coming back here without the others."

"I'll take any chance to be alone with you…" I straightened. My eyes widened, and I motioned to the dogs just as Sassy darted toward the fence yipping her silly little head off. The larger dogs followed, Shutterbug's deeper bark joining the Yorkie's.

A squeal next door was cut short. A man raised his voice. The neighbor's house grew silent.

Brock put a finger to his lips and slowly rose to his feet. Taking my hand, he pulled me toward the house, snapping his fingers for the dogs to follow. It took some convincing to get Sassy to come, but the other two obeyed right away.

Inside, we split up to make sure all doors and windows were locked and lights turned off before meeting up in the living room. Brock pulled his gun from the suitcase he'd stashed under the sofa. I pulled mine from my purse. I'd never fired the thing outside the shooting range and hoped I wouldn't have to.

"Do you think they followed us? Are they here

for us, or should we check on the neighbors?" My breathing quickened.

"I don't know yet. Relax and let's see what happens."

I nodded, keeping my gaze on Shutterbug who stayed between me and the front door. Brutus watched the back. Sassy ran around like a terror, yapping until I thought my ears would bleed. Ruthie really needed to get her dog trained. "Hush, Sassy," I hissed. So much for a quiet night.

A shadow passed outside the front window, sending all three dogs into attack mode.

Brock pulled me to the floor. "Stay down. I'm going to try and see who it is."

"Be careful." I reached out for him, but let my hand fall. We needed to know whether the person outside was friend or foe, although I didn't think a friend would be sneaking around. The dogs definitely didn't behave as if the person outside was friendly.

Brock parted the metal blinds. "Two men in hoodies. Can't tell if they're the same ones we saw at the casino or not." He crawled back to my side. "If your grandmother's dog doesn't shut up, I'm going to open the door and sic her on those guys."

I gave a nervous giggle. "Maybe you should." I scooted until my back was against the sofa. What were the two men waiting for?

Shutterbug's growl deepened.

The front doorknob turned.

Chapter Nineteen

Since I'd locked the door, no one could enter without a key. Shutterbug launched herself forward, slamming against the door. Someone cursed on the other side.

Silence screamed for several seconds before the butt of a pistol slammed against the front window. I gasped and squeezed the trigger, blowing a hole in the front door. Shutterbug yelped and cowered.

Footsteps thundered down the sidewalk.

I scrambled for the door and peered out the hole I'd made. No blood, no bodies. Good. I'd scared them away without killing anyone. My hands trembled, and I placed my gun on the floor next to me before I shot someone I cared about, or my foot.

"Are you okay?" Brock sidled up next to me and pulled me into his arms.

"I could have killed someone." I buried my face in his shirt.

"You pretty much destroyed the door." His chest vibrated with laughter.

"It's not funny." I pulled back. "We should probably check on the neighbors." Things had been quiet over there after the screech and loud voice. What if our assailants had gone there first? A case of having the wrong address? My mind traveled in dozens of directions, none of them good.

Brock helped me to my feet. "Leave the dogs here. If those men come back, they might think we're still here if they hear barking."

I nodded, retrieved my gun, and followed him out the back door and through the gate. The overgrown shrubbery provided plenty of cover as we made our way to the neighbor's front door. It opened on my knock. I cast a worried glance at Brock and pushed it open further. "Hello? We're your neighbors. Everyone okay?"

This was where the heroine became the prey in horror flicks. Hello? As if the killer would actually answer. Since the neighbors also remained silent, things weren't promising.

"I'm going in first." Brock stepped in front of me.

"And let something happen to Hollywood's Golden Boy? No way." I pushed back in front.

"Seriously?" He frowned. "I'm the man here."

"You're the most valuable."

His eyes flashed. "Don't ever let me hear you say that again." He stepped in front of me and barged inside.

No one shot at us, so my foolishness seemed even more stupid. I couldn't blame my ridiculousness on anything but plain old fear.

The house seemed in better shape than the one Ruthie had rented. Clean carpet, if a little thin, brightly painted walls, simple but comfortable furniture. Goodwill and yard-sale decorating with pride. I smiled, remembering the days when my father first joined the police force. Our furniture had been much the same.

A groan came from the back of the house. We hurried into the kitchen.

An overweight man and woman sat gagged and tied to kitchen chairs. The man's forehead sported a lovely purple goose egg.

I shoved my gun into the back waistband of my pants and knelt to untie the woman while Brock worked on the man. "Are you okay? Are you hurt?" I slowly peeled the duct tape from her mouth.

"Two men broke in here and threatened us." She narrowed her eyes. "Are you Canyon? Because if you are, you need to hide. You're the one they're looking for."

"They found us." I'd been right about the idiots getting the wrong house. "They're gone now." I untied the dish towel around her wrists.

"This is a nice neighborhood," the man said, standing and shaking his legs. "We don't need riffraff here."

"We're only renting for the weekend." And would lose our security deposit because of the window and door.

"They aren't riffraff, honey." The woman folded the towel and set it on a mustard-yellow counter. "They're actors."

"Same thing in my book."

"Can I give you something for your trouble?" Brock glanced from the man to his wife.

She said, "autograph" at the same time the man said, "five hundred dollars."

Brock smiled. "I'll do both."

He paid them via Paypal and signed one of the dish towels with a permanent marker while I signed a napkin, then we stepped back outside. "You shouldn't have given them money," I said. "He took advantage of a bad situation."

"It's fine. It won't break me, and they could use the money." He slipped his arm around my waist.

"Kelly." Ruthie's frantic voice drifted over the fence.

"I'm here." I stepped around an oleander bush.

Ruthie smashed into me, wrapped her thin arms around me, and squeezed. "The window. The door."

"We had some visitors. So did the neighbors, but we're fine now." I returned her hug, then stepped back. "I think I'd like to go home."

She gave a sad smile. "Me, too. This isn't the weekend I planned."

"Don't you want to find out who sent the thugs?" Brock glanced over to where Morgan approached. "We could leave the house and check into a cheap motel somewhere?"

"Asking questions of our suspects will fill in some blanks," Morgan said. "I agree with heading home. I don't want Ruthie in any more danger."

Lisa, who looked a bit shell-shocked, raised her hand. "I, uh, wondered…do you guys go through this often? Sitting behind a computer is a lot safer than running around with this group."

I laughed. "You get used to it."

The neighbor woman stepped to the edge of her porch. "Since you're talking in my front yard, I can't help but overhear. Does the name Doyles or Rossi mean anything to you?"

I whirled. "Yes. Why?"

"Because other than your name, we heard those."

I changed my mind about Brock's money. The woman deserved every cent. "Thank you. That answers our question nicely. We're going home."

"My husband called the authorities, so you'll have to answer their questions or get out quick."

Right. The police. Hopefully they'd show up by the time we packed. I couldn't skip out and not file a report.

By the time we'd been interrogated by law enforcement, who didn't seem to believe much of what we told them even though we told the truth, morning arrived. My eyes were gritty from lack of sleep and I closed them the minute we got into the van and headed toward home. I didn't wake up until we pulled into our driveway.

Random screen shots from the last few weeks whirled through my mind like an old-time movie reel. My subconscious was trying to tell me something. The next step in solving the murder maybe? I placed a quick call to Lori, who promised to swing by at the first opportunity.

The moment our group entered the house, they shuffled to their prospective rooms. Except for Lisa, who promised to do more digging on our suspects, but preferred her safe, boring apartment to our crowded, potentially dangerous mansion. In the aftermath of last night, I didn't blame her.

Once in my room, I relented and let Shutterbug on the bed with me. Normally a big no-no, but having her close gave me a sense of comfort and safety. I lay flat and stared at the ceiling, playing the movie reel again in my head.

Hilga and Rossi cheating at poker, two thugs trying to break into our rental, a secret baby, Lana and Mildred pointing fingers at Cheryl as the killer…around and around. I bolted to a sitting position. Lance Cruz was adopted. What if the handsome newcomer to Hollywood was the secret baby? What if Robert was his father? So…who was the mother? I needed to talk to Lance.

The doorbell rang, sending Shutterbug launching off the bed. I opened the bedroom door, and she tore down the hall fully prepared to destroy anyone on the porch. When she stopped the noise and wagged her tail instead, I knew the person outside was friendly.

"I heard you had some excitement last night," Lori said, entering the house. "Sorry about the doorbell. I left my key in my other pants."

"Not a problem. I slept on the way home. Coffee?"

"That would be wonderful." She plopped onto the sofa and rubbed my dog's ears.

I moved to the kitchen. Considering Lori wore jeans and a simple purple tee-shirt, she wasn't working that day. If the worry lines between her brows meant anything, it probably meant she felt stressed. I made the coffee and carried two mugs to the living room, handing her one and sipping the other. "Rough time at work?"

"Girl, you have no idea. Chief Foster is a tyrant. Demanding long hours until we find out who killed Robert Doyles. The gambling movie producer isn't the only crime in the city, you know." She sipped her coffee. "What did you want to talk about?"

I went over what I'd thought about in my bedroom. "Is there any way of finding out who Lance's biological parents are?"

"The files are probably closed, but if I can get a warrant to open them, then maybe." She sighed and propped her feet on the coffee table. "I'm not sure you're headed down the right path, though. My gut tells me Rossi is the guilty one. Your visitors last night confirm it. CSV cameras caught the faces of your two visitors. Thugs for hire, used by Rossi on more than one occasion." Her expression hardened. "They weren't paying you a social visit, Kelly."

"I figured that out for myself." I sat in the chair opposite her. "Do you really think pursuing Lance is a waste of time?"

"Not exactly." She smiled. "If anyone can turn over a rock and scare out the scorpions, it's you. It's uncanny this gift you have. Just don't—"

"Go by myself, I know."

"Ruthie doesn't count. She's the same as going by yourself."

I laughed. "Please don't tell her you said that."

"Too late." Ruthie stepped up behind Lori and crossed her arms. "All the yakking out here woke me up."

"We aren't being loud."

"Well, I woke up to use the bathroom and heard you talking. So stop yakking until I get my coffee." She returned a couple of minutes later. "I want to go with you when you question Lance. Morgan can escort us, if that's okay with our jailer?" She shot a sharp glance at Lori.

"My brother definitely counts as not going alone. Take Shutterbug too."

"Why aren't you at work?" Ruthie sat in the chair across from me.

"I deserve a day off once in a while, don't I?" Lori tilted her head and raised her mug to her lips. "I have one slave driver, I don't need another."

"Did something happen at work?" I asked.

"Why do you ask?"

"Because your voice doesn't sound very convincing about the day off." I raised my eyebrows.

"I'm suspended." She shrugged. "Don't worry. It's just a slap on the wrist while the chief shows off his feathers."

"But why?"

She laughed. "Because I told him every partner I've ever had, including the latest chief-of-police, were dirtier than a white jackass in the mud. He took it to mean I thought he was the latest dirty ass."

"Isn't that what you meant?" I grinned.

"The jury is still undecided. Until Kevin's killer is found, I'm not trusting anyone in the department other than myself and Jason."

"Why not be a little more subtle?" Brock

suggested joining us. "Have a small dinner party here and invite Lance. He'll be more relaxed than if we converge on him like piranhas."

Was everyone in the house eavesdropping on our conversation? "Aren't you sleepy?" I brushed a curl out of his eyes.

"Exhausted, but I went to the bathroom—"

"And heard us talking," I said. "Seems to be the pattern." I turned toward my grandmother. "Ruthie? Are you up for a dinner party next Friday night?"

"I'm always up for a party." She clapped.

Chapter Twenty

Ruthie didn't do anything simple. With the nice weather, she planned a pool party eerily similar to the one where Robert had tried faking his death. Although the party was just as fancy, she kept the number to a manageable one hundred instead of twice that.

"This isn't the intimate dinner party I thought it would be." I wrapped a brightly flowered sarong around my waist. "And why Hawaiian-themed?"

"Because it's fun, and I haven't done that theme yet this year." She patted my cheek and bustled for the kitchen, her white knit cover-up flowing behind her.

How she managed to put together a party of that size in less than a week astounded me. Instead of acting, she ought to be running a mega corporation. She planned the menu, sent out invitations via snail mail and social media, and decorated the place…all without the help of a party planner. Any heavy work went to Morgan, and Sarah just needed a handwritten list of foods to prepare. Amazing. Me? I pretty much hung out with Lori or Lisa, planning our next step in solving the mystery.

Lisa had texted last night that she might have found a hole to climb into and dig up some dirt. She'd let me know at the party. I hoped it would be something to get us over, under, or around the wall we'd hit.

"Stop dawdling," Ruthie called. "Guests are arriving."

I pinned a silk hibiscus into my hair bun and hurried for the pool. Rather than have everyone track through the house, they were to enter through the side gate where tiki torches and flickering multi-colored lights welcomed them. A speaker hidden in a plastic rock played sounds of the ocean waves lapping against shore.

"Aloha." I placed a silk lei around Leo's neck.

"Aloha." He turned to a pretty young brunette on his arm. Since his wife had left him months ago, Leo had someone new on his arm every time he appeared socially. Young hopefuls wanting a break in show biz.

I turned as Lance entered alone. "Aloha. No plus one?"

"Aloha." He smiled, snapping the gum in his mouth. "Not tonight. I want to mingle, not be tied to anyone's side."

"Smart man." I couldn't help but wonder why such a handsome young actor would attend a party alone when there was little chance of meeting single women. Ruthie always invited couples. She wouldn't be happy to have an empty seat at our table. Wait.

I quickly dialed Lisa and told her she had to be here. More snooping online could wait. Problem solved. My freckle-faced, red-haired friend would be ecstatic to find out who she'd sit next to.

"Aloha, handsome." I placed a lei around Brock's neck and kissed him. "You're late."

"Strangest thing. I had to bring the truck. The tires on the Mercedes were flat. Slashed."

"What?"

"Yep." He tapped his finger on my nose. "We're close, sweetheart. Be careful."

"You too." I was the one who always got the warnings. What changed with this case?

I greeted Lana, escorted by actor, David James, who'd played my father earlier in the television series. Handsome, but at least twenty-years older than she. I shrugged. None of my business. My eyes widened at the sight of a made-up Mildred. With makeup and her hair out of its customary tight bun, she was actually pretty. I didn't recognize the man next to her and was surprised that Ruthie had invited the housekeeper.

"Mildred asked to come," Ruthie leaned over and whispered. Uncanny how she could read my face so well. "Since she's one of our suspects, I didn't see any harm in inviting her. Cheryl's also here helping out in the kitchen."

I jerked back. "Is that wise? What if she poisons our food?"

"Sarah will keep a close eye on her, no fear."

All our suspects together in one place. All except Rossi, and he was sure to have someone there to do his spying. I'd keep my eyes out for the person acting nosier than myself.

When it looked as if no more guests were arriving, I strolled around the pool deck. Smiling guests with hands holding glasses of adult beverages chatted amongst themselves. A few surrounded Lance, but not as many as I'd thought. Where was Lisa?

Ah. Sitting alone on the patio, her arm around Shutterbug's neck.

"What are you doing?" I asked, plopping down beside her. "It's a party, not a school dance. You're no wallflower." She really wasn't. She'd straightened her red hair, leaving it to hang in a crimson cascade down her back. Skillfully applied makeup lightened her freckles. "You look very pretty."

"Lance Cruz is here. I have such a crush on him."

"Great, because you're seated next to him at dinner."

"What?" Her eyes widened. "You can't do that to me. I'll be tongue-tied or say something about what I've found on the internet."

"Something good?" Hope leaped in my chest.

"I know who—"

Ruthie stood on the patio and hit a brass gong, signaling everyone to their assigned seats for dinner.

I seized Lisa's hand. "Come on. You'll be fine. We'll talk again later."

She pulled back. "I know who Lance's parents are. There's no way I can keep that a secret. Or I at least know his father."

I planted a hand on each of her shoulders and stared into her face. "Tell me."

"Robert Doyles."

"Don't say a word. I mean it, Lisa. Now we need to find out who the mother is. No clue?"

"She's from Pasadena, I think. At least that's where Robert was when the child was conceived. After that the trail grew cold."

"You are a true genius." I linked arms with her and led her to the table where she became instantly speechless at a welcoming smile from Lance.

"You must be my companion for the meal," he said, removing the gum from his mouth and placing it in his napkin.

She nodded and lowered herself without taking her eyes off him, almost missing the chair. Face as red as her hair, she righted herself.

I spun away to hide my smile. It wasn't hard to recognize attraction when I saw it, and Lance was smitten. Hopefully, he wasn't our killer.

Mildred kept glancing at our table, a worried expression on her face. I had yet to see her take a single bite of food. Could she be worried about Cheryl, who carried trays of plates to the guests?

Pasadena, huh? If Ruthie hadn't invited so many people, I could have come up with a party game where everyone said where they grew up. I couldn't imagine speaking with everyone and outright asking. If I asked only women between ages of thirty-eight and forty-five, that might narrow it down enough. But this was Hollywood. Discerning a woman's true age was next to impossible.

"Tell us about yourself, Lance," Ruthie said. "You're the new kid on the block."

He pulled his gaze away from Lisa. "I grew up here in Hollywood. I was adopted at birth. Played football in high school. Always wanted to be an actor. And to find out who my biological parents are, so here I am, killing two birds with one stone—so to speak."

I spewed my pomegranate tea across the table. "Sorry." What a coincidence. Killing two birds, huh. "Really? Are you having any luck?"

His shoulders slumped. "Not really."

"Is that why you decided to attend the party alone?"

He nodded. "Without having to keep someone company, I could focus more on the job at hand, you know? I think my biological parents might be part of the Hollywood scene."

"Why do you think that?" Could he possibly know more about this case than I did?

"Something my adoptive mother said." He smirked. "After a high school play, she let it slip that it was only natural since Hollywood ran in my blood."

"You should have Lisa help you," Ruthie said. "She's a whiz on the computer. Can find out anything."

Lisa's eyes widened and she shook her head. Lance turned his attention back to her. "Really? Would you help me?"

Her mouth opened and closed a few times, then

she gave a slight nod. "I can try."

"This is turning out to be a great evening. What's the first thing we do?"

The look in Lisa's eyes bordered on terror. "Uh, make me a list of what you do know, I guess."

"I was born a boy. That's about all I know. The job won't be easy, but I think spending time with you might make it worth the headache."

She blushed.

I clutched Brock's hand under the table. I wasn't very old myself, but seeing Lisa stutter and stammer made me feel a lot older.

The guests slowly finished eating and once again formed groups around the pool or dessert buffet. Still holding Brock's hand, I mingled, searching out women in the age range best suited to be the unwed mother of Lance.

"You look like a shark searching for prey," Brock said. "Fill me in."

I told him who I was looking for. "If they're also from Pasadena, that puts them higher on my list."

"Morgan's from Pasadena. Why not ask him if he knows anyone here?"

"Because he's older than most of the…oh." I turned until my gaze landed on Mildred who stood talking to Lance and Lisa. "That means Mildred is from Pasadena, which explains her interest directed at our table during dinner. Mildred is Lance's mother." I whirled, then made a dash for her table, snatching her water glass before the busboy could take it away. I quickly hid the glass under my sarong as Mildred frowned in my direction.

"Go get some DNA from Lance," I hissed at Brock.

"Okay?" He laughed. "That's something I never thought I'd hear outside a movie script until a year ago. Meet me on the side of the house." He headed for the table, palming Lance's napkin in his fist.

I made a detour through the kitchen to grab a paper bag from Ruthie's stash under the kitchen sink. I wrapped the water glass in a paper towel and dropped it inside before joining Brock outside.

He'd located Lori among the guests, and we turned over the evidence. "I'll try and pull some strings to get a rush job on this," she said. "There are a few people who owe me a favor or two." She glanced from me to Brock and back to me. "You two be careful. I saw a couple of men here I didn't recognize. They arrived after dinner. I don't think they received an invitation."

"Rossi's men?" My blood chilled.

"It's very likely." She handed the bag to Jason when he joined us and gave him the name of a gal at the station's lab. "Rush job. I'll call her later."

He nodded and left through the gate.

Lori whirled back to face me. "Let me show you the two men. We may need to have them removed from the property." She led us back to the pool area. "There. By the gazebo."

"Those are the two men who followed us from the poker room at the casino." I'd recognize their square heads and barrel chests anywhere. "You're right. I don't think they're invited."

Lori motioned for Morgan to join us, and the four of us headed for the gazebo. The two men stared stonily at our approach, then walked past us without a word, exiting the property.

"Well, that was easy." And strange.

"They were here merely to observe." Lori narrowed her eyes. "I doubt they learned anything to worry Rossi. You were more focused on Lance than anything else. Maybe this will get Rossi off your back."

"Is he still your number-one suspect?"

"Not in Doyles' death, but he is in your father's."

"What did you find out?"

She led us away from the guests. "I found some documents in the archives at the station before the chief suspended me. Rossi was suspected of paying off police officers. Your father wrote the report saying that Rossi had approached him, offered him a large sum of money, which he refused. He also stated in the report that he suspected Rossi of laundering money. I think Rossi put a hit on Kevin. I intend to prove it and send the man to jail."

I was right. Every mystery I became involved with over the last year was linked in some way to Dad's murder.

Chapter Twenty-One

Which put me right back on Lana's tail. I headed to where she refilled a champagne glass under a fountain. With a firm grip on her arm, I dragged her off to the side. "Where did you find Mildred, and how much do you know about Rossi?"

She blinked like a baby sloth. "What?"

Okay. I needed to dumb things down for her, especially since I was asking about two potentially separate things. "Let's start with Rossi. Don't tell me something I already know. Tell me something I don't."

She tried to frown, but her botoxed face remained impassive. "My husband owed him money. I…give Rossi what he wants…"

"Does he know about the money you stashed away?" I narrowed my eyes. "He must. Everyone else does. Rossi didn't kill Robert, did he?"

"No." Her shoulders sagged. "Rossi is my uncle.

That's why he lent Robert the money he needed. My husband wasn't the only gambler in the family, but Rossi gave him a lot. Now, he's finding ways to recoup."

"By cheating in Vegas with Hilga Smithwick?"

She shrugged. "I guess. I don't follow what he does." She clutched her stomach. "I'm not feeling well. It started before I arrived at the party, but the cramps are getting worse. I need to go home."

"Why pretend you're Rossi's mistress?"

"He doesn't want people to know I'm his niece because I married outside the family's blessing. Are we finished?" She paled, and perspiration broke out on her forehead.

I caught her as she toppled forward. "Someone call an ambulance." My mind leaped to poison. What do you give someone who might have been poisoned by cyanide? Milk? Charcoal?

I glanced at the gathering crowd around us. "Did someone call?"

"I did." Morgan shoved his way through the throng, receiving a sharp look from Mildred as he pushed her aside. He scooped Lana into his arms and raced for the front of the house.

I ran on his heels with Lana's escort, David James. "Did you stop on your way here to eat anything?"

"No," he said. "If we had, I'd be sick too. We came straight here from her house."

We stopped and waited for the ambulance. Sirens blasted in the distance, and I prayed they'd arrive in time. "How was she acting in the car?"

"Complained of a headache and her cheeks were

a bright pink. I thought she'd just used a heavy hand with the makeup or was being dramatic again. Now I feel bad." He sagged against one of the front pillars.

"Don't be silly. Who was at the house?"

"Just Mildred. She said Cheryl had left about an hour earlier."

"Cheryl?" She should have been here with Sarah all day.

"She said she forgot something, rummaged around in the kitchen for a few minutes, then dashed out the door." His gaze locked on Morgan and Lana. "I didn't pay much attention to anyone other than Lana."

The ambulance stopped in front of the house. David climbed into the back with Lana, leaving Morgan free to return to the party with me.

"Do you think it's cyanide?" I asked him.

"I'll be surprised if it isn't." He stopped as Mildred rushed toward us.

"Where did you take her? Why wasn't I informed so I could go with her?"

"She's on her way to Cedars-Sinai. You can meet up with her there." A muscle ticked under Morgan's left eye.

"What is wrong with you?" Mildred took a step back. "Did I do something wrong?"

"I don't know. Did you?"

"Are you insinuating that I harmed Lana?" She smacked his chest. "Why would I? She's my employer. I have a good life working for her. Why ruin it?"

"You tell me."

She groaned, then spun around and stalked away, calling for her date to give her a ride. Once she left, I turned to Morgan. "You know something."

"I only suspect." He led me to a secluded part of the yard. "I'm not sure about any of this, but I've been doing some digging. Mildred might be Lance's biological mother."

"Why do you think that?"

"He looks like her, for one. It started to click when he talked about his reasons for coming to Hollywood. Mildred did the very same thing at his age, but she wasn't able to make a go of it. What if it wasn't because she lacked talent, but because she got pregnant?"

"Lots of actresses have babies."

"But they don't start their career pregnant." He tilted his head. "I don't have all the pieces, but they're starting to fit together."

I agreed. "Okay, but why kill the father of her child? Why Lana?"

"Those are the missing pieces."

With the collapse of Lana, the party-goers dwindled away until only our core group remained. We sat on the patio furniture, nursing our drinks. I'd have to ask Lisa to put a rush on digging up whatever she could find on Mildred, but she'd have to keep the information away from Lance. We couldn't tell him unless we were absolutely sure.

"I just can't figure out why," I said. "If Lance is Mildred's son by Robert, why commit murder? Why not relish in her son's success, even if in private? It doesn't make any sense."

"That's what we need to find out," Lori said. "I'm going to switch my attention from her to the deceased. That's the best way to find out why she might have killed him."

"Or not," Ruthie pointed out. "This is all speculation at this point. Don't forget Cheryl." She motioned her head to where the younger chef removed dishes from a table. "She had opportunity and motive for both Robert and Lana."

I explained about her showing up at the house for a few minutes when Lana was getting ready to leave. "You should question her, Lori." I glanced up as Sarah stepped outside. "How long was Cheryl gone this afternoon?"

"When I sent her out for missing ingredients? Over an hour." Her eyes flashed. "I should have had plenty of sugar, but an entire five-pound bag had been dropped outside and burst open. It took a while to clean that up to prevent an ant invasion. So, I sent Cheryl to the store."

Lori shot to her feet. "Who would have taken the sugar other than Cheryl?"

"We were the only two people here as far as I know. If she dropped the bag, it wasn't an accident. Someone carried it outside on purpose."

Which gave Cheryl a reason to head home. "Did you see a receipt?" I asked.

"Yes, she did stop at the store." Sarah handed an empty tray to a passing young man hired to help clean up. "Funny thing, though. I found the sugar because the back door was left open. The gate, too. Cheryl, of course, denied any of it."

I waved Cheryl over. Sarah took the plastic bin

of dirty dishes into the house.

Cheryl glanced around our group. "What now?"

"Have a seat, Miss Downs." Lori motioned to the seat she'd just vacated. "This won't take long."

That's the first I'd heard Cheryl's last name. I really needed to do my own digging rather than wait for someone to fill in the blanks.

"We're aware of you leaving this afternoon to purchase sugar. Why did it take you over an hour to return?" Lori asked.

"I stopped by Lana's to grab my favorite carving knife. Why?"

"Seems strange that a chef would forget an important cooking utensil."

"In Cheryl's defense," Ruthie said, "she's not a very good chef. No offense, sweetie."

Cheryl huffed. "I'm not the norm, for sure. Is this about the missing sugar because I did not take it from the cupboard and dump it outside. Why would I do that?"

"For an excuse to leave?" I suggested.

"I'm not a prisoner here. I could have left anytime I wanted." She glared around the circle. "Do you seriously still think I killed Robert? Unbelievable."

"You had motive," I said. "He wouldn't leave Lana and marry you. Now, with Lana possibly poisoned—"

"What?" She bolted to her feet. "Someone poisoned Lana?"

"We don't know that." Lori shot me an exasperated look. "She did leave the party because of feeling ill."

"That's why all the questions. You think I went home to poison her just like Robert. Well, look somewhere else. I have a cushy job with Lana, despite our dislike for each other. A nice roof over my head, good pay, and she puts up with my lack of experience because the man she—we—loved asked her to. Killing either one of them would be like slitting my own throat. Stupid. I'm getting a lawyer." She stormed into the house.

Just like that, all questions stopped. It didn't matter. I believed her. My focus shifted to Mildred as the number-one suspect in the deaths. All I had to do was find her motive.

"Let's switch gears." I waved Lori back to her seat. "Is it reasonable to think Mildred might have killed Robert because he dumped her when he found out she was pregnant? It seems far-fetched to me, considering over twenty years have passed."

"Maybe she's held a grudge all these years, and something made her snap recently," Brock said. "Like a trigger that sets off a serial killer."

"We need to find out what that trigger was," Lori said. She glanced up as Jason returned.

The grin on his face told us he had news. "I don't have DNA, but I do have a fingerprint match off Mildred's glass."

"We know it's her glass," I said.

"But you didn't know she's in the system." His smile didn't waver. "She was arrested here in Hollywood over twenty years ago for shoplifting baby formula."

I sat up. "Robert married Lana a year ago, right? Does anyone know when Mildred started working for her? Did she recently move here from Pasadena?" My money was on the same time he married Lana. But where had she lived until then?

Ruthie snapped her fingers. "Right around the time we started filming the first episode of our show, there was a write-up on him in the *Hollywood Tribune*. Susan Gilroy might be able to get us a copy of that article. At the very least, it would have let someone looking for Robert know where he was."

"Who has a cell phone?" I held out my hand.

Lori dropped hers into my palm.

I dialed Susan's number and pressed speaker. "I need a copy of an article you did on Robert Doyles when *The Hart of Crime* started filming."

"Kelly?"

"Yes, it's me. Can you get it?"

"Whose phone is this?"

"Detective Lawrence's. Can you get it?"

"Not until tomorrow, but yes. What's going on?"

"I'll explain when I can. Power up the printer, girl, because you're about to have the story of a lifetime. Just remember…the book is all mine, though."

"You help me get a Pulitzer-worthy article, and you can have whatever you want. I'll call you tomorrow. On your phone." Click.

"Let's go see Lana in the morning and find out when she hired Mildred."

"If she's still alive," Ruthie said.

Chapter Twenty-Two

Lori informed me via text in the wee hours of the morning that Lana Doyles passed away from cyanide poisoning shortly after arriving at the hospital. After reading the text, I sat on the edge of my bed and cried. I'd failed to find a killer before he or she struck again. While my heart and head told me Mildred was the culprit, I had no proof other than a gut feeling. Still, for me, that was enough to confront her. I hadn't acted on my instinct. If I had, Lana might be alive. I intended to remedy the nonconfrontation as soon as possible.

Ruthie and Morgan had plans for the day to visit bakers, having hired Staletti as the caterer for the wedding reception. Brock was filming until late in the afternoon. I had a couple of free hours ahead of me and smiled at Shutterbug. "It's you and me, girl. Lori said I could take just you as a last straw in not being out alone."

Her ears perked up, and she retrieved her leash

from the doorknob.

"Let's get in our morning jog first, then we'll track down our suspect." I ruffled her hair and slipped my feet into gym shoes. Ten minutes later, we hit the sidewalk. Rather than make our way to the jogging track at the park, I chose to be a nosy neighbor instead.

I might not have known Lana long, but her death left a pain in my chest. I couldn't help but feel responsible in a way. How had my father dealt with death so often during his career in law enforcement?

I increased my speed, my shoes slapping the pavement. I'd gone horribly wrong somewhere. Why had Lana kept two women she obviously disliked living under the same roof? It made no sense. Robert was dead. He wouldn't have known if she'd kept her word about retaining them on staff. There had to be something we were missing.

I rounded the corner in time to see Iris Beacon withdraw her head from over the fence. Of course. Nothing happened around there she didn't know. I called her name and waited for her to reappear.

"Kelly." She smiled.

"Good morning, Iris. I have a question, if you've a minute."

"I always have time for you, dear."

"When did Lana Doyles hire her housekeeper, Mildred?"

Iris scrunched her lips. "It was right after she married Robert, if my memory serves me well. It seemed strange at the time. I always thought he knew Mildred before he hired her. There was a certain tension between them that didn't seem appropriate between boss and employee. Why?"

"Just curious. Thanks." I circled around and jogged back home. As usual, I received more information from Iris than I'd asked for. Wonderful. The police department should put Iris on staff. They'd catch their guy nine out of ten times in record time. As I turned down my driveway, I sent Lori a text letting her know when Mildred started working for the Doyles.

Are you out alone? She replied.

Nope. I'm now at home. I added a smiley face. *Next stop is The Tribune.*

Wait for me. I'll pick you up in thirty minutes.

Fine by me. I needed a shower and something to eat before facing Gilroy or the editor, Larry, for that matter.

By the time Lori arrived, I wore stylishly ripped jeans, an oversized shirt, with Shutterbug waiting patiently next to me. I glanced at my reflection in the window. Ruthie would be proud of my fashion sense. Although casual and bought under duress after one of her many lectures on dressing like a star, I looked the part, although my outfit cost an outrageous amount.

Since my dog didn't like apricots, I didn't worry too much about her being poisoned, and I wouldn't eat anything I didn't see prepared. If we stopped at Staletti's for lunch, I'd take my chances there.

Lori pulled in front of the house and honked. "I'm driving," she said out the window as I approached. "I love the Camaro, but don't feel like an adventure on the road today."

"Something else happen?"

"The chief is riding my behind again after Lana's death. He's put me back on the job and demands I find the Hollywood Cyanide Killer." She grimaced. "Yes, that's what they're calling the perp."

I put Shutterbug in the back. "All those silly titles do is feed the killer's ego."

"I know that and you know that, but the public relishes those titles." She drove out the gate and turned toward downtown. "After we talk to Gilroy, I want to pay a visit to Mildred. Oh, and you were never here with me. I told the chief you weren't involved."

"Got it." I grinned. Silly man. Chief-of-police or not, he was no match for two determined women. "If he arrests me for obstruction of justice, I'll just bail myself out. Onward, Lawrence." I pointed to the road in front of us.

"Bail won't always be an option, my friend."

"Then I'll worry about that if, or when, it happens again." Last time I was arrested, Jason risked his job on the force by "letting" me escape. Then I spent a few weeks living under a bridge with Susan, who later became our chef. Life took some interesting turns at times.

We parked in front of *The Tribune* office and went inside. Larry glanced through the window of his office, scowled, then marched toward us. "No dogs allowed."

"She's a service dog." I smiled. "This is Detective Lawrence. We're here to speak with Susan."

"She's in the archives."

"Thanks. No need for an escort," Lori said. "Kelly knows the way."

I kept my grin in place and headed through the cluster of desks. Phones rang, voices rose and fell, computers filled the dimly lit room with sections of light. Sometimes, I missed the ambiance of a news office, even if some of the stories leaned a bit from the truth. Journalism held a special allure for me.

"Don't tell me you miss this place." Lori glanced around. "It smells worse than the precinct, the furniture is decades old, and everyone's as old as crypt keepers."

"Just the reporters. The photographers are young and hip, like me."

"Gilroy isn't old."

"She's the exception." I pushed open a door that read, "Employees only" and led the way through a breakroom to another door, and down a flight of cement steps. There, we found Susan digging through boxes, her smooth hair a mess and her clothes streaked with dust. "Hey."

She shrieked and whirled. "Don't do that."

"Sorry." I wasn't. "Do you have the article?"

"I can't find it. It should be in this box, but it isn't. The file is completely gone."

"What about your computer?"

She plopped onto a stack of boxes. "The one I wrote the article on crashed months ago. There should have been a hard copy of the article in this box. Sometimes I have the worst luck."

"Would someone else have it on their computer?"

"Larry would, but I don't want to ask him." She

raised a dirt-streaked face. "He'll ask too many questions."

"I'll ask him," Lori said. "I can get a warrant if I need to. Let's go, Kelly. Susan, you return later so he isn't more suspicious than he already is."

"Good, because I can't go out there looking like this. What if someone sees me?" She sucked in a deep breath. "Don't forget to fill me in on this, Kelly. We made a deal."

I gave her a thumbs-up and followed Lori back up the stairs. She left me standing outside Larry's office with the door closed. She came back out a few minutes later. "We'll have to get a warrant, but I found out enough. The article came out right before Mildred showed up in Hollywood. She could have seen the article in almost any grocery store."

"How do you know when Mildred arrived? I had to ask someone."

"I'm law enforcement. We can simply look it up. To get further confirmation, ask Lisa to check when she applied for the job, rented an apartment—something concrete that puts her here at the time of that article."

I pulled out my phone and sent a quick text. "Done." I'd check with her in an hour. "Where to now?"

"Lana's."

We drove to the home of the deceased Mr. and Mrs. Doyles. Lori parked and we stared through the front windshield at the house. Such a place of sorrow and turmoil. Of immorality, lies, and deceit. I appreciated my wacky grandmother and loyal Golden Boy more than I could ever express. I pushed open my door. "Ready?"

"Yep." Lori led the way to the front door and rang the bell. When no one answered after a minute, she rang it again.

Another minute and Cheryl answered. "Come on in." Red rimmed her eyes and tears stained her cheeks. "Sorry. Things are a bit chaotic around here. I can't find the paperwork about the bank account Robert left me."

"Sorry for your loss." I curled my lip. "Where's Mildred?"

"She didn't show up today. No need to. We have no employer anymore." Cheryl headed for the kitchen.

"Did you check the guesthouse?" Lori asked.

"No, that's her private space. You can risk her wrath and go knocking, but not me. I like my head on my shoulders, not being kicked around the yard." She stormed down the hall and slammed the door behind her.

I raised my eyebrows and glanced at Lori. "She seems more upset over the lost account information than the death of her boss and the man she loved."

"I'll never understand some people. Let's visit Mildred."

With Shutterbug nosing around the bushes along the flagstone pathway, we headed for the guesthouse at the far edge of Lana's property. Lori knocked. "Mildred? It's Detective Lawrence. I'd like to ask you a few questions, please."

I stepped to the side and cupped my hands around my eyes to peer through the front window. The curtains were drawn, but I caught a partial glimpse of a tidy little room with a kitchenette. Perfect for guests, but kind of small for a long-term resident.

When no one answered, I reached around Lori and turned the doorknob. The door swung open. "I think I heard someone say to come in."

"Fruit of the poisonous tree. It's your mission in life to get me in trouble." She complained, but followed me inside.

I stood in the middle of the small room. A short hall branched off on our right. I didn't need to be told it was the bedroom and bath, since I could see the living area and kitchen. I veered to the right.

Yep. A bedroom containing a small closet, a queen-size bed, and a dresser. Another door led to a small bathroom with a shower, pedestal sink, and a toilet. Mildred must really have had an agenda to live here for a year. Of course, she did seem to spend most of her time in the main house, so it couldn't have been too bad.

I got on my knees and peered under the bed, then between the mattress and boxed springs—anywhere someone might hide something. From the front room, cabinets opened and closed as Lori searched. All I wanted was one little sign to tell me why Mildred would murder Robert, then Lana.

Not finding anything under the bed, I moved to the closet. No shoe boxes, lots of empty hangers. It didn't look as if Mildred planned on returning. So much for finding a clue. If she'd packed up and left, she would have taken anything incriminating with her.

My phone buzzed. A text from Lisa read she'd

discovered something and didn't want to tell me via text. I replied that we'd meet at her apartment in less than thirty minutes.

"Gotta go," I told Lori, racing out the front door. "Lisa has something for us."

Shutterbug glanced up from under a bush and barked.

I switched direction. I could always trust my dog. If she didn't follow a command, there was a good reason why.

A hole big enough for a shoebox beckoned. Next to it lay a gardening shovel. Whatever evidence she might have left here was long gone. Still, I couldn't keep a grin from my face. Innocent people didn't dig holes and flee. Only killers did. I pushed to my feet as my phone buzzed again.

Don't come. She's here. Sent information to Morgan and erased.

I stared at Lori. "Lisa's in trouble." I shoved my phone into my back pocket.

Chapter Twenty-Three

Lori flipped on the lights and sirens and we sped toward Lisa's apartment. My heart lodged in my throat. Not only was Lisa my makeup artist, but my best friend. I had so few of them, other than Ruthie and Brock. I cut a sideways glance at Lori. I could consider her a friend. If I'd known she was dating Dad back when he was murdered, I might have thought differently, but now...I was mature enough to recognize how wonderful she was.

I put a hand on her shoulder. "I'm glad my father had time with you."

She smiled. "We did have some good times." She glanced my way. "I'm sorry we never told you, but Kevin didn't think you were ready for another woman in his life."

"I probably wasn't." I sat back and gripped the handle near my head as Lori careened around a corner before screeching to a halt in front of Lisa's apartment building.

"Which floor?" Lori shoved open her car door.

"Second. Room 203." We thundered up the outdoor concrete stairs and came to a halt outside her partially opened door. The lock had been shot off, leaving behind splintered wood.

Heads poked from open doorways until Lori shouted that she was a police officer and to go back inside.

"Someone was shooting a gun," an elderly woman in a pink-flowered housedress said. "Multiple times." She slammed her door.

"Let me enter first," Lori ordered, stepping in front of me.

"Then hurry up. Lisa could be dying." I pressed against her back.

She shot me a frustrated look and stepped into the apartment. "Lisa?"

"She isn't answering."

"Really? I didn't get that. Stay outside."

"No." I rushed down the hallway, calling my friend's name.

As I dashed from one room to the next, it occurred to me that the only signs of a struggle came from the kitchen/living area. I hurried back to see Lori standing in the center of the room studying the carpet.

"What is it?" I asked.

"No drag marks made by feet. So, if Lisa isn't here, then she had to have left on her own two feet."

"No blood." Thank God. "Just a knocked-over lamp and some cushions on the floor as if she spotted Mildred and tried getting away. Shutterbug was nosing around the pantry. I darted to him and yanked open the pantry, pulling out rolls of paper towels, garbage bags, and toilet paper.

Lisa lay curled in a ball, her arms wrapped around her head. She blinked up at me. "I told you not to come."

"Are you injured?" I helped her to her feet, then supported her weight to the sofa.

"I fell and hit my head when I panicked." She sat. "I spotted Mildred out my window. When I saw the gun in her hand, I grabbed my phone, texted you, and caught my foot on the leg of the coffee table. Did you call Morgan to get the information I sent him?"

"No." I sat next to her, not liking the size of the purple goose egg on her forehead. "All I could think about was getting here."

"If you're up to it," Lori said, "why not tell us what you discovered as I drive you to the hospital?"

"I'm fine." Lisa put a hand to her head. "Not even bleeding." She glared at the coffee table. "She took my laptop."

"You still need your head looked at."

With Lisa grumbling about the loss of her computer and the cost of hospitals, we made our way slowly down the stairs and settled her into the backseat. She leaned her head back and closed her eyes. "Lance is definitely Mildred's son."

"How do you know if the records are closed?" I shifted sideways to watch her over the back of the seat.

She laughed, then paled and put a hand to her head again. "I'm a genius, remember? The records were opened. My guess? Robert paid someone. I still had to dig, but both Robert's and Mildred's names were on the birth certificate. The original simply stated baby boy. The certificate issued at adoption showed Lance's name and his adoptive parents. Place of birth, Pasadena, California."

"Good work." Lori glanced through her rearview mirror. "You sent a copy of those certificates to my brother?"

She nodded. "He responded that he received them and will make sure they're put somewhere safe."

"Back to Mildred." Lori turned her attention to the road. "I'm guessing she shot your door open?"

"I was already in the pantry."

"Good thing you're tiny," I said. "It really was the only place for you to be. I'm surprised Mildred didn't think to look there."

Her eyes widened. "Didn't you notice the paper products in front of me? She would have seen them first and thought nothing out of the ordinary."

I laughed. "I was in such a hurry to see if my hunch was right, I didn't notice. You were brilliant."

Lisa sobered as we pulled into the drive of the hospital. "Drop me off here. You need to get to Lance. Mildred was muttering to herself that it was time she reunited with her son." She pushed open her door. "I can handle checking into the ER."

Lori seemed torn, then finally decided on doing her job. "Kelly will stay with you. I'll get to Lance."

"I want to come." I frowned.

"Meet up with me once Lisa is settled." Her tone brooked no argument. "I've got Shutterbug. She can't go in the hospital."

Growling, I exited the car and followed Lisa into the building. It wasn't that I wasn't concerned, but seeing her up and walking, well…reaching Lance now became top priority.

"Seriously, Kelly." Lisa took a seat at the check-in desk. "Go help Lance." Her cheeks darkened. "We have a date Friday night. I'd like that to happen."

I gave her a quick hug. "Be safe. I'll let you know what transpires and do my best to save your man." I spun and rushed for the door. Outside, I realized I had no vehicle. Sneaky Lori. I searched the lot and caught sight of Susan Gilroy interviewing a doctor near a round concrete table. I made a beeline for her and grabbed her arm.

"Come on. I need a ride, and you'll get a story." I yanked her away from her interview.

"Wait." She tottered after me on ridiculous three-inch heels. "I'm working."

"It's quite possible Lance Cruz has found his birth mother, and she's a psycho who killed not only Robert, but Lana. Is that intriguing enough to pull you away from Doctor Gorgeous? Where's your car?"

"I can interview the doctor anytime. My car's over here." She raced toward a black Honda Civic. "Where to?"

"Oh, uh, I don't know where Lance lives."

She grinned. "I do. I know where all the up-and-coming stars live. It becomes useful in my job."

"Of being a pest." I hooked my seatbelt.

"That's the pot calling the kettle black." She veered onto the main road and sped to the edge of the city limits, parking in front of a two-story, L-shaped complex. "I was actually surprised that rich boy, Lance, lived in such normal surroundings, but then I heard through the gossip vine—that is, Iris Beacon—his parents said if he was going to pursue acting *and* look for his birth parents, he'd do it on his own dime."

"Iris truly is a treasure of information." I climbed from the car and waited for Susan to lead the way.

"Hold on." She quickly changed her heels to flat canvas shoes. "I'm not going out gumshoeing with you ever again in heels. Too hard to run."

"I hope we won't have to this time." I flashed her a grin and waved her ahead of me.

Wearing shorts and a sleeveless top, tousled, sexy Lance opened the door. He wiped a hand towel across a sweaty brow and smiled. "Nothing better to interrupt a workout than two lovely ladies. What's up?"

"You alone?" I peered into the messy apartment.

"Yep. Excuse the mess. I'm used to someone cleaning up after me. Come on in." He swiped a pile of clothes onto the floor and motioned for us to sit on the dark brown leather sofa.

"You haven't had any visitors?" I couldn't believe we'd beaten Mildred to his apartment.

"I wasn't home until half an hour ago." His brow furrowed. "Why all the questions, Kelly? You seem upset about something." His gaze settled on

Susan. "Aren't you that reporter for *The Tribune*?"

"Guilty as charged." She balanced her elbows on her knees. "I'm not here for an interview, just giving Kelly a ride."

"This is all weird, and one of you needs to tell me what is going on. I'm starting to get worried." His eyes widened. "Wait. Did something happen to Lisa?"

How sweet. He already cared enough for her to be one of the first people he worried about. "She did have a break-in and suffered a head injury, but she'll be fine." I folded my hands. "I don't know how to tell you this without it being a bit of a shock, so I'm just going to blurt it out." I took a deep breath. "Robert Doyles and Mildred Carson are your biological parents."

He sat stunned for a moment, then said, "Okay, but why the grim tone? It's not a surprise that Doyles is my father, since he was such a big deal in this town, but who's Mildred?"

"Lana Doyles' housekeeper."

"All right, I still don't get why you're here."

"Because Mildred killed your father and Lana Doyles, attacked Lisa, and we think she's coming for you next."

"To kill me?" His frown deepened. "Why? We've never met. Why did she kill the others?"

I shook my head. "I don't have all the answers, Lance, but we need to go. We can't sit here and wait for her to arrive. I don't think she's going to kill you, but she's not exactly stable in the head, if you get my meaning."

"All right. Let me get changed. Where are we

going?"

"My place. We've got enough security there to foil anyone." I pulled my phone from my pocket and texted Lori. *Where are you? I'm at Lance's with Susan Gilroy who gave me a ride, no thanks to you. No sign of Mildred.* I returned the phone to my pocket.

Lance rushed to the bedroom and slammed the door. Seconds later, the sounds of banging and grunting came from the other side.

"I'm going to use the restroom," Susan said, moving down the hall. "I'm not taking any chances of getting caught with my bladder full."

I sprang to me feet and knocked. "Lance? Are you alright?"

"Yep. Can't find a pair of clean jeans. Be right out."

Lance really needed to hire a maid. He could probably afford one. "We need to hurry. Just grab something. You can wash it at my house."

"If only you were going to your house."

I spun and stared into the barrel of Mildred's gun.

Chapter Twenty-Four

Mildred looked as if she'd been stuck in the drier too long. Her hair frizzed from her usual bun, her clothes sported more wrinkles than a wadded sheet of paper, and black bags hung under her eyes. "Fetch that nosy reporter. We'll wait out here for my son."

"Then what?' I held up my hands. "Kill the three of us?"

"Just you two women. I wouldn't harm my blood." She rapped the barrel of the gun on the bathroom door. "Come on out." Then she did the same on the bedroom door.

"I said I'd be right—" Lance yanked the door open. His eyes widened.

"Hello, son." Mildred smiled. "I'm your mother. Let's get acquainted on the car ride, okay? I've a couple of things to drop off."

I could guess what those couple of things were.

Good thing Susan changed her shoes because it looked like we'd be running.

Mildred pulled some zip ties from her pocket and ordered Lance to bind our hands. "Make them tight, dear."

He nodded and stepped up to me. His gaze clashed with mine.

I held my hands in front of me, motioning for Susan to do the same. "It'll be fine," I whispered. "Follow my lead when we reach our destination."

"No talking, please." Mildred glared. "Let's walk to the van outside. Do not make any sudden moves or alert anyone that you're being abducted."

"Is that what you're doing?" I smirked. "I thought you were marching us to our death."

"Son, I don't want to tie you up, so if you don't want one of your friends shot, don't try anything foolish. Once you get to know me, you'll love me, I'm sure." She motioned us ahead of her.

Wackier than a three-eyed bat. I cut a glance at Susan's pale face. "Sorry I asked for a ride."

"I should know what happens when someone gets around you. Still, if I make it out alive, I definitely have a story to write."

The barrel of the gun poked me. "Shut up."

"Language, Mildred." I glared over my shoulder. "Why'd you kill Robert? If you're going to kill me, the least you can do is fill in the holes."

"Because he left me pregnant and alone."

"Really? You aren't the first, Mildred. Other unwed mothers don't go around killing the baby's father."

"My son is a star," she spit. "I can't let his

father's unwise choices affect his career."

"I'm pretty sure the world is going to find out."

"By then we'll be in Mexico."

"Why Lana?"

"Same reason. Stop asking questions." She opened the back of a rented panel van with the company's logo plastered across the side. "I'll try not to drive too rough." She shoved me inside. My phone fell out of my pocket and slid away. Mildred told Lance to sit up front with her and slammed the door, casting us into inky darkness.

"Now what?" Susan asked.

"We look for an opportunity to run." I stretched down and untied my shoelaces, then pulled one lace through the bottom of the zip tie, then tied it to the other lace. I started sawing my legs back and forth until the zip tie broke. Once free, I felt around the floor for something to cut the tie around Susan's wrist.

"What are you doing?" She hissed. "Are you free?"

"Yep. Saw a video on You Tube on how to escape zip ties. Just in case." I couldn't find anything to help us, so crawled over to Susan and tied her shoelaces together. "Saw your legs back and forth."

"I'm wearing a skirt!"

"It's too dark for me to see anything." I rolled my eyes. "Do you want out of here or not?"

"Of course."

"Then pull up your skirt and work on it." I scooted back against the side of the van.

"If I'd known I'd be kidnapped, I wouldn't have

worn a pencil skirt. Great. I ripped my hose."

"You still wear hose? I didn't think anyone did."

"They make my legs look fabulous. Why are we talking about this? Aren't you scared?"

"Yeah, but this isn't my first time. I'll get scared if my plan doesn't work."

"What's the plan? Yay, I'm free." Susan crawled to my side.

"When that door opens, act like your hands are still bound," I said. "Then, once you're on the ground, run like hell away from the van. Personally, I'm hoping she's taking us into the woods. More cover there."

"She has a gun, Kelly."

"Hopefully, Lance will take care of that little problem." If he paid attention, he could knock her arm away before she squeezed the trigger. "If we get separated, keep running. I'll find you eventually."

"I don't like this plan. Too many things left to chance."

"You have a better one?"

"No." Her voice dropped.

"Then this is our plan." I'd try to come up with a plan B, but didn't hold out much hope. I closed my eyes to catch some sleep before the final act of the day.

The van took a sharp curve and sent Susan and me rolling to the other side. A rude awakening indeed. Mildred was an evil witch. My head slammed against the metal panel. Ow.

"I'm going to kill her with my bare hands,"

Susan muttered. "The biggest story of my life and I'm going to be black and blue."

I shared her sentiment. My cell phone. Where was my cell? "Find my phone."

The van rumbled to a stop. A car door slammed.

"Never mind. It has a tracker. Get ready for the plan." I sat against the wall and stared in the direction of the door. "Remember. When I run, you run. No hesitation."

"Got it." Susan's voice trembled.

The doors opened, blinding me. When my sight returned, I saw we were indeed in the woods. Mildred was going to shoot us and leave us to the animals. Really? Ahead rose Mount Shasta in all its majesty. We'd been driving for quite a while. That was the direction I'd run. Miles of forest to disappear in until I could find a way to connect with Lori.

Keeping my hands clasped together, I let her drag me from the van. The moment Susan's feet hit the ground, I screamed Lance's name, shoved my shoulder into Mildred's stomach, and started running, then glanced over my shoulder.

Lance had a hold of Mildred's arm, forcing the gun to face upward. "Go!"

"Let go of me, son." Mildred struggled.

"No, mother. It's just the two of us now."

Susan's eyes were impossibly round as she rocketed after me. "Don't look back."

I couldn't help myself. I cast one more glance at the fight behind me before diving into the brush and saying a prayer for Lance's safety. Not hearing a gunshot gave me hope, and I stopped for a second to catch my breath.

"Why are we stopping?" Susan crouched next to me, her chest heaving.

"To give Lori time to find us or Lance the chance to control his mother. I'll take either one."

The gun went off. I shot to my feet in time to see Lance clutch his side and fall. Mildred had shot her son. Whether by accident or on purpose...I wasn't waiting around to see. Grabbing Susan's hand, we sprinted through the trees. I'd have to rely on Lori finding us.

We couldn't run around like lost chickens. We needed a place to hide. Lori would come, and she'd bring the cavalry with her. We just had to survive long enough.

A primal scream from behind us sent birds shooting into the sky. The hair on the back of my neck stood at attention. On second thought, maybe Mildred shooting Lance was an accident. She'd blame me, I felt sure.

"There." Susan pointed to an overhang on a hill. "Maybe we can keep her from climbing up to us." Forgetting the modesty she'd shown earlier, Susan hiked her skirt to her waist, giving me an unwelcome sight of her bottom, and started climbing.

"A little warning, please."

She glared at me. "I work hard to keep fit. It can't be that horrible."

Whatever. I reached up and gripped a branch. It pulled free from the dirt, sending me sliding down the few feet I'd managed to obtain. "I'll find somewhere else and keep Mildred's attention off you. If you get the chance, head back to the van and get help." I darted down a narrow trail, almost obliterated by Mother Nature's attempt to reclaim what must have once been a hiking path.

I stopped at the edge of a cliff. With a quick glance behind me, I dragged my feet as if I'd gone that way, then took care to walk on rocks and leaves rather than dirt as I headed away from the cliff. Maybe half a mile further, I came across a shallow creek and splashed my way upstream until I found a place where roots hung thick over an embankment. I ducked inside and sat hugging my knees. Mildred was tracking me for sure. I was out of options, but I'd done all right thinking on the fly. If only my luck would hold.

"I'm coming for you." Mildred's voice rose over the sound of birds singing and the creek babbling.

Her footsteps sounded above my head, but I couldn't see her. She'd crossed the creek somewhere. I held my breath and hugged my knees tighter, then relaxed when the steps faded away.

Memories of living under a bridge with Susan came back. I didn't want to die in the woods anymore than I'd wanted to die there among the garbage. All because of one man's bad choices. Now, not only had he been murdered, but also his new wife. The one he'd left Susan for, thus starting her temporary decline into homelessness. I would never let anyone have that much control over my life. From this moment on.

I pushed to my feet and peered out of my hiding place. Night was beginning to fall. I was alone and weaponless. There was nothing to do until morning. If I couldn't see, neither could Mildred. Maybe she'd give up during the dark hours of the night, and I could find my way to safety.

Resting my cheek on my knees, my mind drifted to Brock. He had to be frantic with worry. If I knew my man, he wouldn't stop until his strong arms wrapped around me. I smiled. Maybe I did want someone to have some control over me. Brock would never misuse that power.

A twig snapped nearby. I froze, my ears straining. No further sound came, and my shoulders released their tension. The only way Mildred could find me now was with a flashlight, and I'd see her coming from a long ways away.

Chapter Twenty-Five

I woke to the sound of sobbing. "Susan?" I peered from under the roots to see her hunkered down on the edge of the creek.

"Oh, my gosh." She threw herself at my chest, knocking us both into my little hidey-hole. "I thought you were dead. When I woke up and it was dark, I knew you had to be dead or you would have returned. Then I got lost." Her sobs increased.

I put a hand over her mouth. "Shh. We won't be easy to find here, but if you keep up that racket, she'll know where we are. You were supposed to go for help." Dumb girl.

"I got lost."

I bit my tongue, realizing some people were directionally challenged. "Maybe Lance managed. Maybe he's still alive."

"What now?"

"We stay here as long as we can." I had no

desire to put myself out there for a bullet to find. If Mildred discovered our location, then I'd leave.

"Do you think the creek water is safe to drink?"

I shook my head. "I wouldn't risk it." I leaned my head against the dirt wall behind me. My stomach growled, and my mouth felt like I'd gnawed on cotton. Thirst and hunger might drive us from our hiding place before Mildred could.

"No more. I don't care about any prize." Susan glowered. "No more following you around and putting myself in danger."

I shrugged. "Then you don't want it bad enough. There's nothing like first-hand experience."

"I'm not on a crusade to find my father's killer." She rolled her eyes. "Don't look so shocked. Everyone knows why you feel compelled to solve these crimes." Tears rolled down her cheeks. "I'm sorry. I don't mean to be so…mean. I'm tired, hungry, thirsty, and scared. I want to go home."

I wanted to promise her we would, but clamped my lips shut. That wasn't a promise I could keep, no matter how strong my desire.

After the sun had been up for an hour, I crawled from our hole and glanced around. Maybe Mildred had taken Lance to Mexico as promised. It had been about ten hours by my calculations, since I last heard her voice. I waved Susan forward, then put a hand to my lips.

She nodded in understanding and joined me on the creek bank.

Squaring my shoulders, I followed the creek back the way we'd come, using as much foliage as cover as I could. When we reached where the van had stopped, I peered through the thick branches of bush.

Lance sat propped against the wheel well, his shirt soaked with blood. His head hung low over his chest. From where we were, I couldn't tell if he was alive or dead. I started to head for him when a crashing in the brush behind me made me freeze.

Shutterbug jumped on my back and licked my neck. She wiggled so hard and whined so much, I couldn't help but laugh.

"My sweet girl. You found me." I wrapped my arms around her neck. "Let's go help our friend, okay?" I stood and glanced around for Lori. "Where did you leave the others?"

Keeping a cautious eye out for Mildred, but knowing Shutterbug now had my back, I raced to the van, then knelt next to Lance. I felt for a pulse in his neck. He stirred under my touch.

"She took the keys," he whispered weakly.

"Help is coming. See? Somebody had to have brought my dog." I motioned to Shutterbug.

Her hair bristled. A growl started deep in her throat.

"Hello, Kelly." Mildred stepped from the trees. "I knew you'd come sooner or later. You have a soft heart." Her gaze settled on Shutterbug. "Since your dog is here, help isn't far behind, so I'd best hurry the job along."

I stood and faced her. "After finding your son, why wouldn't you have gotten him medical attention? That's what a good mother would do."

"We all know I'm not a good mother. If I was, I wouldn't have given my child away." She heaved a heavy sigh. "I was going to remedy that, but you ruined any chance I had. Go ahead and line up next to Lance."

"Can I ask you something before you shoot me?"

She nodded.

"Did you sneak into our kitchen and steal a bag of sugar?"

She laughed. "Clever, right? That put the target on Cheryl's back. Now, where's that reporter?"

"Right behind you." Susan raised a branch as thick as her wrist and brought it down on Mildred's head. The woman fell.

Shutterbug barked and stood over the woman. I grabbed the gun. "Get something to stop the bleeding," I told Susan.

She removed her suit jacket and pressed it against the wound. "How bad is it?"

"Just a graze," Lance said, "but it's bled more than I like."

"Hold on." I put a hand on his shoulder as Lori and two police officers stepped from the trees. "The cavalry has arrived."

I sat on the patio, sparkling water in hand, and leaned against Brock as Lori sat across from us. "Good news, I hope?"

She nodded and smiled. "Lance and Mildred

will both be fine. She'll go to jail for a very long time, and he'll have a scar to impress Lisa with."

I chuckled. "Looks like their date night will be in front of the television, taking it easy on his stitches."

"I don't think they care." She accepted a beer from Sarah. "I've never seen two people fall for each other so quickly."

I smiled up at Brock. "It didn't take us long."

"Once you realized I wasn't just another playboy." He tapped my nose.

"What happened with Cheryl?" I asked, turning back to Lori.

"She's gone. Cleaned out Lana's file cabinet, leaving most of it on the floor of the office. Looks like some clothes might be missing from Lana's closet, along with Robert's safety deposit box. Small fish. None of Lana's accounts were messed with. She must have found what she needed. Unless someone presses charges, there's no crime committed that I know of."

"Lance must be distraught."

"Maybe, but Lisa will soothe his aches. It can't be easy finding out your birth parents aren't anything like you thought they'd be." Lori raised her bottle in my direction. "Another job well done and more gray hairs on your grandmother's head. What's next?"

I grinned. "Finding out who killed Dad."

"I'll have you know there isn't a single gray hair on my head." Ruthie plopped onto a chaise longue and crossed her ankles. "I pay good money to make sure." She smiled as Morgan joined us. "We've decided to get married here, in the backyard."

"You change venues too often for me to keep up." I sipped my water.

"We won't change our mind. We've moved the wedding up to three months from now."

I spewed my water. "If you weren't too old, I'd think you were pregnant."

"Hush your mouth." Ruthie smiled. "I don't want to wait any longer. No more flip-flopping on a wedding date. I can't let this big guy get away."

Brock's hand found mine. He leaned forward and whispered in my ear, "Want to make it a double wedding?"

My mouth dried up. My heart stopped. I sprang to my feet, ran to the pool's edge and jumped in.

Brock followed me, pulling me close and swimming us both to the opposite end. "Not the reaction I'd expected."

"Just a surprise." I wrapped my arms around his neck. "I'd always thought a proposal would be more private. But, yes, Brock Handsome, I'll marry you. But not here, not with Ruthie. I want a beach wedding. Let Ruthie have hers, then we'll have ours. Okay?" I stared into his eyes.

He nodded. "Anything you want." He claimed my lips and we sank out of sight.

The End

Scan the code to check out the last book in the series, To Snap a Killer

Dear Reader,

I hope you've enjoyed the latest escapades of Kelly and her gang. If so, please leave a review. Reviews are worth gold to an author.

Website at www.cynthiahickey.com

www.cynthiahickey.com

Cynthia Hickey is a multi-published and best-selling author of cozy mysteries and romantic suspense. She has taught writing at many conferences and small writing retreats. She and her husband run the publishing press, Winged Publications. They live in Arizona and Arkansas, becoming snowbirds with three dogs. They have ten grandchildren who keep them busy and tell everyone they know that "Nana is a writer."

Connect with me on FaceBook
Twitter
Sign up for my newsletter and receive a free short story
www.cynthiahickey.com

Follow me on Amazon
And Bookbub
Shop my bookstore on shopify. For better price and autographed.

Enjoy other books by Cynthia Hickey

Misty Hollow
Secrets of Misty Hollow
Deceptive Peace

Calm Surface
Lightning Never Strikes Twice
Lethal Inheritance
Bitter Isolation
Say I Don't
Christmas Stalker
Bridge to Safety

Stay in Misty Hollow for a while. Get the entire series here!

The Seven Deadly Sins series
Deadly Pride
Deadly Covet
Deadly Lust
Deadly Glutton
Deadly Envy
Deadly Sloth
Deadly Anger

The Tail Waggin' Mysteries
Cat-Eyed Witness
The Dog Who Found a Body
Troublesome Twosome
Four-Legged Suspect
Unwanted Christmas Guest
Wedding Day Cat Burglar

Brothers Steele
Sharp as Steele

Carved in Steele
Forged in Steele
Brothers Steele (All three in one)

The Brothers of Copper Pass
Wyatt's Warrant
Dirk's Defense
Stetson's Secret
Houston's Hope
Dallas's Dare
Seth's Sacrifice
Malcolm's Misunderstanding
The Brothers of Copper Pass Boxed Set

Time Travel
The Portal

Tiny House Mysteries
No Small Caper
Caper Goes Missing
Caper Finds a Clue
Caper's Dark Adventure
A Strange Game for Caper
Caper Steals Christmas
Caper Finds a Treasure
Tiny House Mysteries boxed set

Wife for Hire – Private Investigators
Saving Sarah

Lesson for Lacey
Mission for Meghan
Long Way for Lainie
Aimed at Amy
Wife for Hire **(all five in one)**

A Hollywood Murder
Killer Pose, book 1
Killer Snapshot, book 2
Shoot to Kill, book 3
Kodak Kill Shot, book 4
To Snap a Killer
Hollywood Murder Mysteries

Shady Acres Mysteries
Beware the Orchids, book 1
Path to Nowhere
Poison Foliage
Poinsettia Madness
Deadly Greenhouse Gases
Vine Entrapment
Shady Acres Boxed Set

CLEAN BUT GRITTY Romantic Suspense

Highland Springs

Murder Live
Say Bye to Mommy
To Breathe Again

Highland Springs Murders (all 3 in one)

Colors of Evil Series

Shades of Crimson
Coral Shadows

The Pretty Must Die Series

Ripped in Red, book 1
Pierced in Pink, book 2
Wounded in White, book 3
Worthy, The Complete Story

Lisa Paxton Mystery Series

Eenie Meenie Miny Mo
Jack Be Nimble
Hickory Dickory Dock
Boxed Set

Hearts of Courage
A Heart of Valor
The Game
Suspicious Minds
After the Storm
Local Betrayal
Hearts of Courage Boxed Set

Overcoming Evil series

Mistaken Assassin
Captured Innocence
Mountain of Fear
Exposure at Sea
A Secret to Die for
Collision Course
Romantic Suspense of 5 books in 1

INSPIRATIONAL

Nosy Neighbor Series
Anything For A Mystery, Book 1
A Killer Plot, Book 2
Skin Care Can Be Murder, Book 3
Death By Baking, Book 4
Jogging Is Bad For Your Health, Book 5
Poison Bubbles, Book 6
A Good Party Can Kill You, Book 7
Nosy Neighbor collection

Christmas with Stormi Nelson

The Summer Meadows Series
Fudge-Laced Felonies, Book 1
Candy-Coated Secrets, Book 2
Chocolate-Covered Crime, Book 3
Maui Macadamia Madness, Book 4
All four novels in one collection

The River Valley Mystery Series
<u>Deadly Neighbors</u>, Book 1
<u>Advance Notice</u>, Book 2
<u>The Librarian's Last Chapter</u>, Book 3
<u>All three novels in one collection</u>

Contemporary

Romance in Paradise
<u>Maui Magic</u>
<u>Sunset Kisses</u>
<u>Deep Sea Love</u>
<u>3 in 1</u>

<u>Finding a Way Home</u>
<u>Service of Love</u>
<u>Hillbilly Cinderella</u>
<u>Unraveling Love</u>
<u>I'd Rather Kiss My Horse</u>

Christmas
<u>Dear Jillian</u>
<u>Romancing the Fabulous Cooper Brothers</u>
<u>Handcarved Christmas</u>
<u>The Payback Bride</u>
<u>Curtain Calls and Christmas Wishes</u>
<u>Christmas Gold</u>
<u>A Christmas Stamp</u>
<u>Snowflake Kisses</u>

Merry's Secret Santa
A Christmas Deception

The Red Hat's Club (Contemporary novellas)

Finally
Suddenly
Surprisingly
The Red Hat's Club 3 – in 1

Short Story

One Hour (A short story thriller)
Whisper Sweet Nothings (a Valentine short romance)